BOURGEOIS BLUES

BOURGEOIS BLUES

a novel by

Lisa Herman

M&S

The publisher makes grateful acknowledgement to the Ontario
Arts Council for their financial assistance.

Canadian Cataloguing in Publication Data

Herman, Lisa
Bourgeois blues

ISBN 0-7710-4074-1

I. Title.

PS8565.E75B68 1989   C813'.54   C88-095069-2
PR9199.3.H47B68 1989

Printed and bound in Canada

McClelland & Stewart Inc.
The Canadian Publishers
481 University Avenue
Toronto, Ontario
M5G 2E9

To Alan, who said keep going.

CHAPTER 1

*I*n the beginning there is the thesis. There is structure: lightness and darkness and a house with a weeping willow on the front lawn and a peach tree in the backyard. In the house are a father, a mother, a boy and a girl. They are eating breakfast: orange juice, egg, toast and cocoa, together a tapestry in a frame, each one a colored thread, woven into and blending with the others, their knots tied securely in place and bounded by solid wood. Each is defined in relation to the others; without them he is no one at all. I, the girl, alone with myself, am lonely to the point of non-existence.

So rigidly defined by day, I people my private world with magic antitheses at night. There is Grace: a combination of Cinderella's Fairy Godmother and Vanessa Redgrave, who takes me up to green meadows, bathed in sunshine, where surrounded by smiling children of striking factory workers, we drink cups of tea in fine china. And more often than Grace, I invite Free. He is dark and sinewy, like Ché Guevara, and he carries me to deep, muddy pits in the jungle where men in camouflage fatigues stroke and fondle me (I'm suddenly sprouting large breasts) and give me courage to strike yet another blow for freedom. I choose where to go. The revolution is inside me, guerrilla warfare from the mountains within.

No one suspects in the daylight world what is going on inside me. A master of subterfuge I fill the waking life with a series of tasks which I perform well. I am an expert at defining expectations and fulfilling them. I excel in school with no effort. I am a good child at home. I am liked by my peer group, invited to parties and chosen for friendships. There are boys who date me and kiss me goodnight and sometimes even write me letters which I save in a box with a blue, striped cover. I know how to drive a car and have held jobs appropriate to my age and education. I am responsible and mature in my outlook. My high school teachers think I will go far but I don't know what that means because in their world there is nowhere I want to go.

I try my best to daydream about wearing a gray, pleated skirt and a white blouse closed at the throat. I try to see myself at some job: tidy and answering questions in a dignified manner, getting a large check at the end of the month. I have a house and a husband and a boy and a girl and we water the lawn with a simple hose, not liking those new fangled sprinkler systems. When something is broken, it's immediately fixed. The children have orange juice, egg, toast and Fry's cocoa for breakfast.

I have charge cards at major department stores and buy things wisely on sale from their catalogues. But there is a sadness in me.

"Are you in one of your moods again?" says my mother. "Why don't you go outside and get some sun on your face? Nobody likes a pale, mean face."

She is in the kitchen, calling to me in my room. She wants to teach me to cook and I won't let her. She wants to teach me how to wear makeup and I won't let her do that either. She, in her own frustrations, is the only person who can guess at my misery and she pretends she doesn't understand.

"Why can't you leave me alone?" I call.

I wait for an answer but there isn't any.

When my father comes home from work he will also shut himself in his room, away from her call to activity. My brother only comes home to eat and then leaves again.

I read a lot: fantasy and science fiction, finding spots of warmth behind the closed door of my room. In summer there are the pools of sunshine that splash through my window, and in winter the warm air from the furnace funnels through the heater. I read about Good and Evil and struggles for Truth. I read a minimum of a book a day.

The phone rings.

"It's for you," says my mother.

Harriet is on the line.

"You want to go to the Plaza? We can get some chips at Coleman's, see who's there. We can look at clothes too, something for graduation. My mom says I can get a strapless. Did yours agree?"

Coleman's Restaurant, across from the Lawrence Plaza, is the neighborhood hangout.

"Naw. I feel too fat to try anything on."

"You're crazy," says Harriet. "If only I could be that thin. So we won't eat chips."

"I don't feel like looking at dresses. Besides, I'm not sure I'm going to graduation."

"What's that supposed to mean? You're on the planning committee. You already told David you'd go with him. How can you not go?"

Harriet is jealous that I'm on the planning committee. The

teachers in charge didn't choose her because she dates boys who aren't in school. I only date boys who are in school.

"Listen, kid," I try hard to keep my voice from being as pale and mean as my face, "don't push it right now. I'll talk to you later."

We say good-bye.

My mother has recharged her batteries from my phone conversation.

"What's this about not going to your own high school graduation? What is happening to you? This is the third or fourth weekend you haven't moved from the house. And what about the pile of university applications I sent away for? At least you could use this time for completing those."

"I'll fill out the one for York. I don't need to do any more. With my grades, I'm already accepted."

I've decided on going to the new York University because parking's easier than at the University of Toronto.

"What is wrong with you?"

It's an accusation, not an inquiry.

"What are you going to do? Sit here until school starts in the fall? If so, then at least go out and look for a summer job, or volunteer for something. There are people you can help who haven't had the advantages you've had. There are people in the world who have much more of a right to be miserable than you do. They have real reasons, like poverty and injustice. When I was your age I was using every spare minute organizing for social justice and world peace. I wasn't lying around the house feeling sorry for myself."

She pauses for effect.

"You'll just get fat lying around like this."

The cruelest blow of all. I yell back towards the kitchen.

"I don't believe in social justice. There never was such a thing and there never will be. You were witness to the invention of the atomic bomb. You were there for the Holocaust. Don't give me that crap that you trust people like the Russians to work things out and it'll be okay after the revolution."

"Don't you use that language with me, young lady. You know more than anybody, as usual. With that tongue and poison face I find it hard to understand what your friends see in you."

I can't argue that one. I slam the door of my room.

But the truth is, I'm no longer so vulnerable to her weapons. I have a plan. I'm going to run away from home, and as much as it's possible to conceive of myself at the age of eighteen as a runaway, I am filled with power. Once when I was nine I ran away. I didn't want to go to Y daycamp and I hid behind a board in the backyard for twelve hours. Nobody found me, and feeling humiliated, I finally came home to pee. At eighteen my range of adventurousness is not as circumscribed. When the final exams are over, I'll file the York application, and then I'm going to San Francisco. I'll take my savings to buy a plane ticket and get a job there to support myself. I'll find an apartment and let them know where I am so they won't worry, and of course I'll be back in time for school. I'm not altogether irresponsible. I am off to San Francisco: a dream name like Camelot or Narnia, a place made for knights and school children in search of adventure.

My father comes home. He puts his briefcase on the hall shelf and passes my room on the way to his.

"Hi," I call through the closed door.

"Hi, sweetie," he says.

He's tired, as usual. He works all week and Saturdays too. When he's home he sleeps a lot. On Sunday mornings, when I was little, I would crawl into bed with them. My father would stroke the hair at the back of my neck and

11

make up stories about wild animals who hid in the flowered wallpaper.

I would like to tell my father that I'm leaving, but we haven't really talked since he stopped telling me about the animals. Sometimes he tells me to try and understand my mother, and that's about it. He's a sad man who, like me, has stopped believing in social justice, both of us a disappointment to my mother.

When I leave, my father will feel he has failed her in yet another area. He might even die of a broken heart, working longer and longer hours to speed the process. Or maybe he will live and hope again, and wrapping me in his long, dark cloak, lift me in his arms and together ride with me on a gray horse to San Francisco. That, of course, is not realistic. He's too frightened to run away. He doesn't have, like I do, my mother's strength.

Still, I wish there was some way to talk to them. I'm scared of things like psychedelic drugs and free sex. I don't even understand rock and roll music. But I need to go away, and in 1969 San Francisco is the place you go to. It's the place where something is happening, and I want to be part of it.

My brother comes home and my mother calls us to dinner. We sit around the kitchen table eating the food too quickly to justify the hours spent preparing it.

"Well, how was the game?"

My mother uses her standard, sprightly, trying-to-interest-a-fifteen-year-old tone.

"Your mother asked you a question," says my father.

"Fine," says my brother.

My mother makes another stab at conversation.

"There are rumors of an invasion into Cambodia. I wouldn't put it past that fascist Johnson. Do you know what the casualty list is today?"

12

She's made a tactical mistake here by not directing her question to a specific potential respondent. No one answers.

So she continues.

"I don't know how decent Americans can go on living in that country."

This time my brother takes the bait.

"Maybe there aren't any," he says.

"Any what?" says my mother.

"Any decent Americans," says my brother.

Having provided more fuel, he can now finish his green beans.

My father and I exchange a glance.

"But of course there are decent Americans," says my mother. "There's an active anti-war movement in the United States and there are some very respectable and intelligent people involved in the protest. It's not all those drug-crazed kids, you know. There are doctors and lawyers and honest, working people. If you'd read the newspapers, perhaps you'd be better informed."

"Yeah, Mom," says my brother, and having finished his beans, leaves.

She glances helplessly and hopelessly at my father and me.

"Am I the only one who cares?"

I answer this time.

"You're the only one who needs to use Cambodia as an issue for dinner-table conversation."

"Do you see how she talks to me? Day in and day out it's like this. Don't I deserve some respect? She's a young woman now, not a child. She acts like a spoiled five-year-old."

My father shrinks as her anger is poured on him. I don't care. He deserves it. I only said out loud what he was thinking.

I stand to clear the dishes and wash them. I'm a good girl; I help a lot around the house, I always do my homework, I bring home good grades, I even read the newspaper. My brother doesn't wash dishes. When he dips his hands in dishwater, he develops a mysterious rash.

In the evening we watch television, first Bonanza with Lorne Greene, who used to be the newscaster, and then the war with the news guy, who used to do the weather. Vietnam is as vague as the ranch in Bonanza, as vague as the civil rights movement and the Holocaust before it. I don't know any war veterans, cowboys, Negroes, concentration camp survivors, fascists or Buddhist monks. My international contacts are limited to my French teacher, who's lived in Europe, and my classmate Megan, who visited England. Death has reached as close as my friend Susan's mother, who died last year. Sin smokes cigarettes at parties and knows boys who drink beer. We let them touch our breasts and no more.

"What would you do if I came home and said I was pregnant?"

My brother gives me a what-are-you-up-to-now look.

My mother laughs. "I'd say, you made your bed, now lie in it." She laughs again.

My father says, "Are you asking seriously? Because if you are, then I want you to know you'd be free to tell me everything and I would do what I could to help."

I smile at him. My mother is hurt. She will never break that closeness between us.

My brother tells us to shut up so he can watch the movie on television. It's *Exodus*, part one, another foreign country with good and evil cleanly defined.

"Somebody left hair in the bathroom sink this morning," says my mother.

If I didn't have the feeling there was more, perhaps I could reconcile myself to this.

And what if there isn't any more? What if I just read too much and see too many movies and life really boils down to hair in the sink?

But if there is a chance of something else, I owe it to myself to check it out. I'm not talented or beautiful enough for life beyond sink hair to come to me. But I can be a regular person caught up in momentous circumstances, like the people on the *Exodus*.

So the decision is really final. I'm going to San Francisco. I will be caught up in momentous circumstances, open up the pages of the world's bestseller and find a phrase about me in there, maybe even a sentence, something to tell me who I am away from these people whose lives are too intertwined with mine. And someday I will honestly be able to answer questions like, "What is your favorite color?" and "What do you like for breakfast?" without having to suit my reply to the questioner.

I drift further away from the movie to make pictures in my head; to a forest where I'm attacked by not-too-fierce dogs. My clothes are ripped off and I'm found by my math teacher. He starts to comfort me and we are soon making love. I know the touch of his skin. When he corrects my work in class he stands close to the desk, his arm touching my bare arm. I'm doing better in math than I've ever done before.

The movie is over and the family says goodnight. We go to our rooms. The house is quiet. The willow on the front lawn weeps.

CHAPTER 2

*T*he Boeing releases me into the San Francisco airport, surrounded by fog and filled with soldiers. I stare at the uniforms, never having been so close to live bodies in the real thing. I remember my father's World War II RCAF jacket that hangs in the hall closet. The men notice me staring and, embarrassed, I grab my suitcase from the carousel and run for a taxi. The driver takes me to the Y for women, where I check in and fall asleep.

Waking on Toronto time, much too early to go out, I lie in bed in the clean but less-than-motel furnished room, and start my research into who I am. It seems a good idea to begin with something positive about myself, and after some thought I remember one thing I like: my hair after it's been washed, how it feels, like soft leaves kissing my head.

Proceeding to analyze the significance of this data, I recall my grade seven health teacher's lecture on kissing, in which she proved to the segregated female class why it was preferable to be a woman than a man. Her conclusive proof lay in the fact that it was nicer to be kissed than to kiss. Therefore it follows that my enjoyment of freshly washed hair, experienced passively like being kissed, is a confirmation of my sexual identity.

Feeling more in control after these mental gymnastics, I dress and emerge a stranger into the empty San Francisco streets. The unfamiliarity shrinks me back into myself, and like Alice, I grow smaller and smaller, wishing for a white rabbit to direct me. Alas, there are no furry animals in the vicinity and I make my own decision to walk in a downhill direction, thus adding another item to my identity list: I prefer walking down to up. I find a tiny snack counter, open to the sidewalk, with five barstools arranged in front of it. A sleepy Chinese man serves me black coffee and a fresh sourdough roll. I ask for milk.

"Next time order cafe con leche," he says.

Continuing down the hill I come to a square filled with grass, trees, chirping early-morning birds and a few people sitting on benches. I sit down next to a kindly-looking old lady who is throwing breadcrumbs to some scruffy-looking pigeons. We gaze together at the universe. A mother, dragging a small child, stops with an irritated shrug, pulls down the child's pants and points him towards a flower bed. Not at all embarrassed, he makes peepee, and I feel a smile growing on my face.

Inside my grin I can feel eyes on me and so look up and into the gaze of a young Negro man in a red, woolen hat.

"How are you, pretty lady?"

"Fine, and you?"

I am proud of myself, answering as I would to anyone, even though it's my first time talking to a Negro.

"Oh, I'm just fine too."

I have trouble understanding his English, but I recognize the accent from television. His face is strange, never changing expression.

"You come here before?" he asks.

"No. This is the first time. I just got to San Francisco."

He sits up straighter and the movement, along with his silent face, make me uncomfortable. I turn to the pigeon lady for comfort, but she's asleep. As I get up to go, he reaches out and grabs my arm.

"Where to, pretty lady? We were just getting acquainted."

I don't want to be rude to him. It would be terrible if he thought I didn't want to talk to him because he was a Negro.

"I've got a lot of things to do today. Got to get going."

He holds my arm tighter. The old lady snores softly.

"Let go now."

He doesn't.

"Hey, I don't like men. You understand?"

It works and he drops my arm. I grin at him and start to back away, but his face is cracking like thin ice over creek water and he stops me with a snarl.

"You white trash are all alike these days. Honey, what you and your sisters need is some black cock. That would fix you up."

His face shuts down again and he gazes frozen into space.

When finally I can move, I creep by the old lady who is again feeding the pigeons and by a mother who is holding a little girl sucking a chocolate cookie. I feel ashamed and dirty in front of these nurturers and run up the hill towards a shower.

I pant my way to the Y. I should return to Toronto immediately. I've made a mistake leaving home, thinking I can hide my frightened, ugly helplessness in a place where no one knows me. Was I pretending to be sophisticated, talking to a strange man? Of course he must have assumed I wanted sex with him. That doesn't depend on color. He was right to be angry with me, smiling and talking and making promises I wouldn't keep. I led him on. I was a prick tease. And what kind of pervert was I, watching a little boy pee?

My legs slow to a crawl. My plan for adventure is fatally flawed, doomed to failure by my sexual identity. I can't leave home in search of excitement like a boy can. My adventure has to have sex as its primal focus. Excitement and daring feats happen around men, and I'll just have to pay my dues to participate.

Perhaps I can find a man to watch over and protect me from the others. Secure and safe, wrapped in his long, flowing cloak, we can ride on the gray horse on our quest.

At the Y a young woman is tacking up a notice – "Roommate Wanted" – on the bulletin board. She's thin and tall, long, black hair, round wire glasses, white Mexican blouse, blue jeans and wooden shoes. Maybe she's Dutch.

"I'm looking for a place."

She turns to interrogate me with her stare, eyes huge behind her glasses.

"It's sixty dollars a month. Are you working?"

Her tone is brisk and business-like.

"No. But I've got some money until I get a job."

She takes the notice off the board and crumples it in her hand.

"There's just one other condition. I call you Snow. I always call my roommates Snow."

"Okay. And you?"

"Taye."

The formal negotiations are ended and she smiles.

"It's best if you get your stuff now, before you have to pay for another night."

We walk several blocks to Taye's apartment, but even though my suitcase is heavy, it doesn't seem far. She talks without interruption, telling me about herself, as if she senses my doubts surfacing after agreeing so quickly to live with her.

She's twenty-five years old, divorced for the last four of them. No children. After her divorce she lived on the Amazon and studied weaving with a witch. She still weaves, but works at other jobs to make money. She prefers that there not be meat in the house, but she can tolerate it, if I insist. The phone costs extra. She doesn't care if I have guests; she enjoys meeting people. Her last boyfriend was a filmmaker. Her husband was an insurance agent and they lived in Seattle, where she grew up. She's had eight roommates in the two and a half years that she's lived in San Francisco.

"Nobody's stable anymore. I don't like to get too close because of that. After the third roommate I just decided to call everybody Snow. For obvious reasons."

"It suits me fine. I'm from Canada."

She nods.

We reach a four-story white building and climb to the second floor. A sign on the door says "Taye and Snow." She opens the door and my first sight is of a large, curved window with a loom in front of it.

"That's called a bay window, even though we can't see the bay through it."

I had forgotten the city was by the water.

The only other furniture is a low table with a stereo. There is a wall-to-wall burnt-orange carpet, boundaried by cushions of various sizes, shapes and colors.

We move quickly through to the Snow room. It is light and airy. A low dark wood dresser stands under the window, a foam-rubber slab covered by an India print is on the floor. Over this is a poster with a monkey sitting on a toilet.

"That belonged to the previous Snow. She moved in with a Reichian analyst."

20

I laugh, understanding that this is a joke, and afraid to disappoint her in her assumption I understand. I ask to see the kitchen.

This room pleases me. The glass-fronted cupboards, the refrigerator on legs, the gas-burning stove and the butcher-board table with wicker chairs all make me feel like I've arrived at the Ponderosa.

"Make yourself a cup of coffee. I have to get dressed for work."

She shows me how to light the stove with a match. I put the kettle on and sit at the wooden table trying to imagine her work clothes. I decide on a granny dress and shawl.

She enters in a mini-skirt and knee-high white boots and senses my unasked question.

"I work in a Volkswagen showroom, handing out bonus vouchers. This is the outfit that goes with the job. Keys are under the mat."

She's gone, and left alone without her directing energy, I realize I don't really want coffee. I turn off the gas, open the fridge and am immediately assaulted by strange leafy greens and crawly sprouts, bottles of violently colored liquids and fermenting mounds of milk products. I decide to buy some food that is recognizable to me and some sheets for the foam slab. Though it seems forever since I left Toronto, it's only eleven o'clock in the morning of the next day.

The streets are crowded now. I pretend that I am Taye and move quickly and purposefully, as if I have a goal in mind. I don't look to either side. I don't stop to loiter. I am careful not to smile or look in anyone's eyes. I'm proud that I'm learning to take care of myself and that I've made myself invisible.

Arriving at Macy's Department Store I feel the revolving doors suck me in like a magnet, to the comfort of a universe of simple needs and gratifications. It is a universe known to

21

me from times of turmoil in Toronto, when I sought sanctuary in Eaton's and Simpsons. My pulse rate slows; surrounded by counters and goods I am at last in familiar territory.

Confidently I buy a set of black-and-white printed sheets and permit myself to browse at the makeup counter. An attractive early-middle-aged client is trying on lipsticks, the flawless saleslady helping her.

"I'll be with you in a minute."

"No, don't bother. I'm just looking. I don't want any help. Just pretend I'm not here."

Why am I talking so much? I don't want human contact and I especially don't want a lecture on makeup. Absorption of information in this area would sabotage my declaration of filial independence. And yet the paints and polishes fascinate me.

The client senses my confusion.

"Excuse me, dear."

What is it about these San Francisco people? I have never before had a stranger talk to me about anything more significant than the time or a bus route.

"You are a lovely child."

She has a deep and comforting voice.

"But you really must do something with yourself. You're not being fair to the real you, going around uncared for like that."

"You sound like my mother."

But I smile at her theatricality and invite her to continue.

"Step over here and let Ernie make you into a new woman."

I stay where I am, not sure I've heard correctly.

"He's a he all right. Don't feel bad for not knowing. Ernie's the best-groomed customer I have. He has a wonderful sense of style. You really shouldn't pass up an opportunity to let him help you."

"Anybody can make a mistake, cookie," says Ernie.

I move towards him as if mesmerized by a snake and blame Simpsons and Eaton's for not preparing me for this experience.

Ernie asks the saleslady to bring eye shadow, liner, rouge, lipstick and other materials that I can't identify, and tilting my face towards his, begins to work. Calling on some inner strength, I relax, agreeing to be his Galatea, and let his gentle fingers mold me. After intense concentration, he stands back and nods his head. The saleslady hands me a mirror and I gasp. The face in there is quite lovely: big eyes, soft skin, vulnerable mouth and looking like there is no makeup at all.

Ernie chuckles and he and the saleslady watch as I look in the mirror, like proud parents showing off their new baby.

"I'll take the lipstick."

It is now Ernie's turn to gasp.

"But you must have it all. How can you not, after seeing who was hiding inside there?"

"What's with you?"

I fumble for my money.

"You get a commission or something?"

His face falls. "Is that what you thought?"

He rallies and turns to the saleslady.

"She's perfectly charming, isn't she? She thought it was all a sales pitch."

He turns back to me, still fumbling in my purse.

"Darling, please, let me buy you the rest of the things. As a present."

I remember the stories in *Confession* magazine of what homosexuals do out of hatred for women and I remember the man in the park this morning, and this time I'm not going to invite punishment and torture out of fear of giving offense.

"Don't buy me anything, thank you. You've been nice. Please, don't give me anything."

I back my way slowly from the counter, leaving the lipstick unpaid for and almost forgetting my sheets, until I can no longer bear their amused faces and run outside. I slow to a walk, and attempt to merge again with the crowd as I search for a market.

I succeed, and hug the sweet face of Chef Boyardee as I negotiate the return to Taye's apartment. Shivering from exhaustion I light the gas stove, heat the ravioli pieces and savor their mushy tomato warmth. Tucked into my new sheets, I fall asleep under the shitting monkey.

Taye's voice wakes me up to darkness.

"Snow, you asleep? Everything okay? I'm making an omelet. You want some?"

I pad into the kitchen, half asleep and not really hungry for food, but starving for a form at least seen twice. I watch her focused, graceful motions. She beats the eggs, adding spices from glass bottles with fat corks, and pours them into a cast-iron pan, letting them simmer as she slices small chunks of yellow cheese into the thickening mixture. We don't talk. Taye runs the omelet under the broiler so that it puffs and crusts, and serves us on white plates with green borders.

"I talked too much this morning."

I nod no.

"I know I did. I was hyper. I'm going to have to talk about it in group this week. I thought I had things better under control."

"Group?"

"My women's group. God, I don't know what I'd do with-

24

out it. My life is divided into two parts, before group and after. You want tea?"

I nod yes. I'm not thirsty but I'm afraid to hurt. What I really want is to go back to my room, shut myself away and sleep.

"Rosehip, camomile, ginseng?"

"Whatever you have."

She might as well have asked if I prefer Donner to Blitzen; they are also names without identities.

"Perhaps something without too much caffeine."

"They're all herbal teas. None of them has caffeine. Don't you know that?"

I burst out crying.

Taye looks like I've stung her.

"Hey, whoa, man. I didn't mean to hurt you. I keep forgetting it's your first day here. You're tired and upset, right? Probably came straight from Mommy and Daddy's house too."

I cry harder.

"Listen, Snow, we're sharing an apartment and that's all. I don't want any more responsibilities than I already have. You're just going to have to deal with your own pain and your own problems. No leaning on me. Each of us with her own limits. You got it?"

I nod and wipe my tears.

"Do you want me to look for another place?"

"No, we'll work it out. You're just tired. Go get some sleep."

"I'll wash the dishes first."

I dunk my hands into the soapy water, lower my head and let the tears plop into the bubbles. Always my sadness has been accompanied by my mother's anger telling me to stop feeling sorry for myself and my father's harmony of guilt and sympathy. But as Taye has made abundantly clear, I am now

25

alone. My actions no longer have context or meaning. I am the thread without the carpet.

Stretched on my foam-rubber slab I think about a possible option for the alleviation of my pain: dying. It's an interesting alternative to life, in that it would also solve the problem of my guilt at causing suffering to others. I had stupidly believed that I could leave my poison vials at home where they were invented, that away from the catalysts, the noxious materials would detoxify. But the ugly contagion is inside me. Only one day in San Francisco, and I've already poisoned four people: the Negro, Ernie, the saleslady and Taye. I have made each of their lives a little darker.

And yet there is still a chance to be an unsung hero. By my suicide I can make the supreme sacrifice and contribute to the salvation of mankind by destroying one of its minor menaces. Taye's gas stove must be a sign that I have stumbled upon the Fates' plan for me. Sylvia Plath style, I will stick my head into the oven.

On the verge of sleep I recount my crimes for the day. I should not have let the Negro believe I was interested in him, I should have bought the makeup from Ernie and the saleslady, and I should have stuck to my decision to return to Toronto, letting Taye find a more suitable roommate.

I know I will dream the Vietnam dream tonight. It is the deserving punishment to me and my kind who cause evil: the sound of the wailing women, the smell of the burning monks' flesh and the napalmed bodies in a pile. Oh, well.

CHAPTER 3

*T*aye leaves a note saying she'll give me "space to get myself settled" and will be back in a week. For three days I don't leave the apartment, don't see another human being; for the first time in my life I stay alone. The only intrusion is the phone, a persistent nasal-toned male who knows to call me Snow. I hang up on him.

I think about calling home, but don't. I think about the gas oven, but don't do that either. I find a set of *Lord of the Rings* and the wizard, Gandalf, finally succeeds in arousing me to action. On the fourth day I start to make a plan.

The first major project is to find a job. This means I must go out and buy a newspaper, which is logically preceded by getting dressed. I am relieved to be thinking again and approach my dresser with a mixture of relief and determination.

I put on my slightly padded bra and the panty hose with the heavy elastic top. These are my compromise solutions to my mother's demand for heavy padding on top and full girdle on bottom. A dark-blue straight skirt and pale-patterned blouse enhance the motif of slim the behind and expand the bust. The blouse is cut long to further cover the offensive protuberance. My shoes have heels and my hair is teased to give height. Dressing is like molding Jell-o.

Suited in my armor, I emerge into fresh air and mid-morning daylight. The Chinese man at the coffee bar remembers me and serves me a sourdough roll and coffee with warmed milk.

"Cafe con leche," he reminds me.

I feel recognized, cared about, and the life force grows a little stronger.

The newspaper stand is next to the coffee bar. At first it's difficult to find the newspapers because of the pornographic magazines. I stand hypnotized by one particular cover: a giant-breasted woman kneels, mouth wide, about to gobble a stiff, black penis. Unable to resist, I signal to the vendor that I want this and a newspaper, and sure I'm being followed by every pervert in the city, I race to the apartment. I stand inside, panting, washed in waves of shame. When I am calmer, I stuff the magazine under my sweaters in the dresser and flopping on the bed, turn my attention to the newspaper.

The headline screams out casualty numbers. The Toronto papers did the same, but here some of the numbers are given names and stories and even a picture. It's different being inside a country at war than looking at it from across the border.

Across the border here is Berkeley, or as the columnist calls it, Berserkley. I'm surprised at his condescending tone, like that of the Canadian papers towards the United States. The protests about the war and People's Park that are taking place in Berkeley are described by him as if they were college fraternity stunts. Are my plans for being at the center of world focus only delusions? Was everything I saw on television in Toronto – the breaking of windows in the banks and the "pig trashing" – was it all just a variation on crowding into phone booths and eating goldfish?

I reach the limits of my capability for disappointment and turn to the entertainment section. Playing right here in San Francisco are both *O Calcutta* and *Hair*. Then I am at the hub of the universe.

Comforted, I pass through commercial advertisements on my way to the want ads: Meditation, Graphology, Healing, Group and Private Sex Therapy. I rest for a while with the restaurants specializing in foods from every country in the world.

The want ads strike me as out of order. I concentrate and realize what's wrong: there is no separation of jobs for men and women. How am I supposed to know to which category the ad applies? I circle the ones that call for typing, knowing these must be for girls. And finally, in a special display box, I find a clear message:

WANTED: INTELLIGENT WOMEN FOR WORK IN EDUCATIONAL MATERIALS Energetic, personable women for work with people. High school graduates. No experience necessary. Training provided. Call for an appointment.

I call. A woman's smooth voice tells me I have reached the offices of GROWTH and I may come in that very afternoon at three o'clock. She gives me the address, which she says is a cable car ride up the hill.

Calling on Gandalf, I shut off thinking processes, straighten my clothes and let the adventure begin.

The cable car is my gray horse. It bucks and whinnies, coaxed into bursts of speed, and suddenly is reined to a protesting stop. If the reins were in my hands, when we reach the top of the hill I would let us swoop in one flying leap to the ocean, suddenly lying sparkling vast beneath us. Though I grew up by the water, this infinite blue makes me uneasy. The lake in Toronto had a frame.

GROWTH's offices are in North Beach, over a sidewalk restaurant where sophisticated-looking people drink wine and eat salads, just like in a European movie.

I find the sign marking the entrance to GROWTH, enter and climb the stairs. Along the wall I find the meaning of life: on the way up are three posters in glass frames, all of children with arms outstretched to sun and flowers. The captions read: "You are the most important person in your life", "Today is the first day of the rest of your life", and "War is harmful to children and other living things." These seem like good thoughts.

At the top of the stairs I open a wooden door and find a carpeted and quiet waiting room with a receptionist who manages to be blond, elegant and natural looking. Five other girls, sitting in white chairs, look up at me.

The elegant woman's eyes find and hold mine.

"Hi. My name is Laurie and I work at GROWTH. You're here in answer to the advertisement."

"Yes."

I make an identity decision.

"My name is Snow."

"Well, Snow."

She doesn't move her gaze from my eyeballs as she, by exquisite instinct, reaches for a paper on her desk.

"You will fill out this application form as a preliminary procedure to your interview. Take a comfortable chair next to the others, Snow, and you can quickly and efficiently fill in the information. If you have any questions, Snow, you can ask me."

Her gaze leaves my eyes and turns to the paper. My hand reaches automatically to take it, and Laurie continues, as if on a pre-programmed course, to concentrate on a filing folder on her desk. Is she a robot? She may be some advanced form of technology that automatically assimilates spoken information. I move to a comfortable chair and continue to watch her.

She is perfect. I can imagine her entire life swirling about her in caressing circles as she bobs to the top without effort. Just watching her fingers move a pencil, the intricate serenity of the motion, makes me feel a pimple under my right cheek. No one would dare to treat this creature with disrespect, yell obscenities at her or ridicule her makeup. If someone did try to cloud her day, he would end up slinking off like an obnoxious child. Her well-oiled gears mesh together; no squeaks. If this is what they're looking for at GROWTH, it's not me.

I check the other girls in the room and, to my relief, find them more normal looking, of assorted sizes and shapes. A tall one stands and moves to the desk, handing her completed form to Laurie.

Laurie stands, her trim body as perfectly assembled as her face.

"We can go right in now, Gloria."

Gloria and Laurie disappear. A new girl comes through the wooden door and Laurie returns to greet her in the identical words, tone and movements as she did me. The girl responds and moves to a comfortable chair.

"Snow, I suggest you fill out the form now."

The new girl and I turn to our application forms.

There are questions about education and experience and who to notify if you die. I lie about who to notify, giving the name and ex-address of my dead grandmother. On the second page, under the title "Motivational Orientation," there is a list of fifteen questions:

31

1. Do you feel the need to change the world?
2. Do you feel there is meaning to life beyond day-to-day coping?
3. Do you get what you want?
4. Do most people not understand you?
5. Do you believe that power corrupts?
6. Do you believe that there are objective criteria for madness?
7. Do you think life controls you?
8. Are you your own worst critic?
9. Do you remember the taste of breakfast this morning?
10. Are you able to say "I like you" when you feel like it?
11. Do you believe in God?
12. Are you alone most nights?
13. Do you believe what people say?
14. Are you able to say "I don't like you" when you feel like it?
15. Did you enjoy filling out this questionnaire?

I answer randomly, half yeses and half nos, and give the form to Laurie.

"Very good, Snow. In just a few minutes you will have your interview. Please sit down, Snow, and make yourself comfortable."

My turn comes, she calls my name, and together we go into a quiet, carpeted room with a long conference table. An older, tailored woman with graying streaks in her hair sits at the head of it. She also finds my eyes and gives me a combination drinking-at-the-well look, with a call to war.

"Mary," says Laurie, "this is Snow. Snow, Mary."

We nod politely.

"Thank you, Laurie," says Mary.

Laurie leaves. Mary motions me to a seat midway down the table.

"Please sit down and feel comfortable, Snow."

She takes my application from a pile, reads it and then looks up.

"Well now, Snow, describe to me what kind of work you're looking for."

"Well, something with people," I say, remembering the ad. "And I'd like to make money at it, of course, and not be too bored."

"Well, Snow, I'll be frank with you. Both your answers on the questionnaire and the impression you make in person are of an intelligent young woman in search of herself. If I am correct in this assumption, I would then say that GROWTH is the right place for you."

There is no welcome in her words. It is simply a recital of a logical equation. I wait for her to continue speaking, but she doesn't. She looks at me, waiting for a response, and I wonder if I am to spend the rest of my life like this, stuck like a bug on a pin. I have to speak.

"Listen, uh . . . "

"Mary," she says graciously, having won the silent battle.

"Listen, Mary, I have no idea what this place is except that I feel very weird here."

She smiles, a tiny quiver of her lip.

"I have no idea what kind of job is being offered, or if in fact one is being offered at all. The newspaper ad said something about educational materials. After spending over an hour of my time in this place, I think I'm entitled to some kind of information."

I am amazed at my courage.

"Slowly, slowly, Snow. Though I must say I do like your enthusiasm. First of all, as I said, if the assumption of your suitability is correct, an assumption that only you yourself can validate, then a job is being offered to you. Secondly, you can rest assured that no one begins work at GROWTH without a thorough introduction to the company from the president, Langley Keel, himself. Our three-day training program will thoroughly introduce you to our materials in preschool education. I'm sure you've heard of Headstart. Like them, we work with parents and young children to provide them with a solid initial base for the future."

Having told me nothing, she waits for me to say yes. And I, without understanding the rules or purpose, enter the contest of wills that is between us. I decide this time I will play to win; and Mary will be the first to speak.

I change tactics, break contact with her eyes and look around the office. In the far corner, away from Mary, is a small table with a metal sculpture on it. I squint to see it better.

"Why don't you take a closer look?" she says.

She's spoken first, but somehow I don't feel I've won.

The sculpture is a black, metal bird cage suspended from a black, metal pole. Inside, a metal man sits on the perch, his hands clutching the iron bars of the cage. His body is distorted, his face agonized. Behind him, and he doesn't see it at all, the door to the cage is open. A chill goes down my spine and I'm scared to turn and face her again. So I stand staring at the metal man.

After a very long time, Mary says, "You're very lucky, Snow."

I turn and her dark eyes comfort me now, say I'm of value and bring me back to the table. It is the gaze of the Chinese coffee man, of recognition.

"I think I'd like to work here."

I don't remember consciously making the decision.

"You're lucky."

She continues as if I haven't spoken.

34

"A new training group is starting tomorrow morning. You'll be able to join it at eight o'clock sharp. Let me stress, Snow, that at GROWTH we are very concerned about meeting responsibilities and commitments, and eight o'clock means eight o'clock. Being on time is a sign of how one keeps one's other commitments. You agree with that, don't you, Snow?"

I nod yes, not sure exactly what I'm agreeing to.

"Then we'll see you at eight, Snow. Bring a bag lunch because we'll work right through until the afternoon. Good-bye, Snow."

She moves her eyes to the next application on her table.

"Good-bye," I say.

She doesn't respond, having dismissed me from her field of interest. I open the door and in a strange, dazed state, walk into the outer office, not really seeing anything.

"Good-bye, Snow," says Laurie as I walk through the outer door.

I am down the stairs and into the street. Life bustles around me: cars passing, voices shouting, the air cool in the early evening. Gradually I become part of it and a voice pierces my isolated time zone.

"Hey, little one. Yes, you. Over here. Two tables to your left."

I see a tall man waving at me from a sidewalk table.

"You don't remember me, do you, love? Come here, darling, and have a seat."

I walk towards him, still caught in that image of the metal cage.

"You're that child from Macy's, aren't you? The one who ran away when I wanted to buy her a present."

It clicks.

"Ernie. You do remember me? What's wrong, dear? Are you on something? Wait," he holds up a hand as if to stop me from speaking, "don't pay any attention to what I just said. I'm not your mother, right?"

I smile.

"See, it's getting better already, isn't it? Now, we'll just buy her a long cool drink and pretty soon she might even be able to talk."

He calls the waiter and orders an iced tea with mint.

"Love, I think you'll need to sit in order to drink your tea."

I hadn't realized I was still standing. I sit.

"Now just relax and enjoy."

I sip the ice-cold drink and finish the return to earth and the reality of Ernie. I'm not scared this time, just curious.

"Why are you being kind to me?"

"I guess that question deserves an answer. The weather is lovely. It's 1969. And, after all, we are in San Francisco."

I sip my tea and watch Ernie, who is watching everybody else. He's wearing less makeup and looks older in the sunlight. He's thin and fragile looking, but balances the vulnerability with a cynical expression tattooed around his mouth. He's elegantly dressed, but this time in more male attire: tailored jeans, a wide belt and a dark-green, wide-necked T-shirt.

"Pardon the appearance, little one. It was a long, happy night."

"Ernie, I still can't figure out why you're talking to me. What do you want?"

He pauses, really thinking about it.

"I don't know. Maybe a friend who doesn't lay trips."

I look down at my almost-empty glass. This man is saying he cares about me, that I'm in some way important to him. I have been seen and remembered, like with the coffee man and with Mary. I don't understand how this can happen with strangers. I was taught to believe that relationships only occur out of structure: home, school, marriage.

"You want to walk a little?" I ask.

We walk down the hill without talking. At my building I touch Ernie's hand. It's starting to get dark.

"This is where I get off."

He takes a pen and notepad from his leather purse.

"Here's my phone number, love. If you feel like a stroll sometime, give me a call."

In the empty apartment I eat and lay out the light top and dark bottom for tomorrow's meeting. The nasal-voiced caller calls and I'm friendlier to him. I'm glad that Taye is not here to pass judgment on my day.

My head full of pictures, sleep comes like the air pockets on my jet flight.

CHAPTER 4

At precisely eight o'clock I see Langley Keel, head of GROWTH, for the first time, and I know I want him. I want him like a kid wants an ice-cream cone. Yearn, covet, desire and pine. They are no longer printed words from a nursing novel, but physical sensations: loss of balance, giddiness, tearing, shivering, inability to concentrate and nausea. My mind becomes obsessed with the desired object: images of touching, talking, delighting in new discoveries. It's like seeing Tomorrowland for the first time, just like it was on television. On the inner screen the new images become merged with favorite old ones: *A Man and a Woman*, *Love with the Proper Stranger*, *Elvira Madigan*. I flash forward, projecting Langley and me through the familiar scenes. First we will recognize the pain of eons in each other's eyes, and then together make it go away for a while, knowing we are safe for the moment. We will choose and be chosen, outside temporal and physical reality, seeing the uniqueness and depths that only we two can perceive. Cosmically fated for this encounter, we will live on a level neither of us has touched before.

There is, however, a problem. As Langley sits on a raised platform, one arm on the back of his chair, one leg crossed at the ankle on the other, I know that he arouses variations of my vision in each of the nine other girls in the room. Graying slightly at the temples, with his slim, hard body, he looks like a cross between Max Von Sydow and Humphrey Bogart. He's comforting father and lonely little boy; knowing everything, yet looking for answers himself. His magnetism is irresistible, and knowing there are those better equipped to entrance him, I sigh and graciously remove myself from the competition.

Mary greets us.

"Young women. You have been chosen from over a hundred applicants to participate in GROWTH's three-day training seminar. During this time we will acquaint you with those basic principles and methodologies that have enabled us at GROWTH to achieve our record-breaking results. Also during this three-day period, as we do in all our endeavors at GROWTH, we will focus on enhancing the growth potential of each of you individually. The basis of all our work here is finding people, such as yourselves, who are in touch with their own potential for change, and providing them with the means to get there. This special initial awareness, that growth is infinite, is a prerequisite for development and is a quality we feel you in this room possess."

She pauses for a minute, catching the eyes in each of our faces arranged below her. From her position on the platform, slightly to the right of Langley, she is even more formidable than she was in yesterday's interview. I have trouble meeting her probing pupils. The other "chosen" in the room look older and more experienced than I do; their clothes are suited to their bodies, their posture and gestures come from some centrally coordinated source. They boldly meet Mary's eyes, and one of them even looks into mine and smiles. She's blond and pretty, but too heavy, and that makes her human and easier for me to smile back.

Mary continues, as if she senses my thoughts.

"Though in the eyes of the beholder, each of the others in this room may seem very content with herself, let me assure you that each and every woman here is dissatisfied. Every single one of you is seeking something more, something better. We at GROWTH are dedicated to helping seekers like you. But you must remember, we think you have potential, but it depends on *you* how well you will use our help. How far you will go in reaching your own potential is your responsibility. Yours alone. The ball, as they say, is in your court. And now, ladies, I give you Langley Keel."

There is silence as he pulls our energies towards him. I'm already prepared for the initial routine as he draws our eyes into his. I meet him and feel the naked orbs lock into sync. Instantly he knows me better than I know myself. There is that promise to unravel the knots and to reveal endless mysteries. He washes me with warmth and caring and extends his invitation to care back. You and I, say those liquid brown pools, can rest and trust here.

"Hi!"

He smiles, crinkling the corners of the dark brown magnets. His voice is slightly gravelly and deep.

"I'm Langley. I'll be with you for the next three days as we cover the material you'll need to begin your participation in GROWTH. But first I want to meet each of you. So say your name and a couple of things about yourself. We'll start here."

He turns to the girl at the left end of our line. She giggles. I switch off and desperately try to think of a sentence that says I'm unique.

I say, "My name is Snow and I'm a thread in search of a carpet."

I immediately feel pompous and foolish. Covered in waves of humiliation, I miss the names of the girls who come after me, except for the blond who smiled at me, whose name is Franny and has finished a year at the University of Berkeley.

Langley remembers everybody. He calls each name and waits again for the eyes to meet him. When the mesh occurs, he moves to the next. Satisfied, he begins to speak, his voice lulling and soothing, as his eyes continue to stroke, to comfort and to bathe. I try to follow what he's saying but the content is jumbled and the words themselves sometimes don't make sense. There is a theme, the life and times of Langley Keel, but constant side trips blur the issue.

He begins with his childhood, growing up in Brooklyn. There are details about various loving relatives inside the walls of his home, and the pressure of tough gangs from without, both of these groups locked in a life-and-death struggle for his allegiance. I listen to his version of *West Side Story*, try to follow, and begin to feel sleepy; sure now that the voice and liquid eyes are purposefully lullabying me in that direction. Words penetrate occasionally: Zen Buddhism, being in the NOW, alternate realities. But I've known about alternate realities ever since I read the C.S. Lewis Narnia books, and I become more drowsy, letting myself drift into the back of the closet and through the hanging coats to the snow-covered land and the smell of Turkish Delight. In the distance I can hear the witch cackle, but I'm not afraid. Aslan is on the move and he will protect me. Faintly I hear Langley's voice saying things like "Power" and "Life Force" and "Individual Responsibility" and it is also the voice of Aslan. A spell of warmth is being cast and spring will come.

"And now we'll break for lunch," says Langley.

I shake myself. It is already twelve o'clock. He has been speaking for three hours.

"Thank you very much for your attention this morning. I know it has been a long stretch, but now that you have the background of GROWTH as an enterprise, after lunch we can move right into your own participation in our organization. I think it best if you stay in our offices and eat your bag lunches here. We'll bring coffee and cold drinks. Be ready to start work in forty-five minutes."

We are left alone, feeling shy and not sure if we've shared the same experience. Have we been through some communal baptism or was it a lecture on business practices? I look at my fingernails, all bitten down close to the fingertips, except the thumbs. I don't bite the thumbs, to preserve the illusion of self-control.

"Well," says Franny, "I am obviously not one to let ceremony stand in the way of food."

She stretches, laughing at herself, and looks for others to join in her giggle. Some do. Being very sensitive to fat jokes, I don't, but say, "Come on. I'll join you. Bring your chair over by the window and we'll get a little air."

"So," she says, munching a giant hunk of red cabbage, "what do you think? He's very beautiful, isn't he?"

My own egg salad has squished through the bread and is soggy to the touch.

"Franny, do you have any idea what we're doing here? I mean, there are definitely details lacking, like what is the work and how much do we get paid."

"Do you have anything better to do today?" asks Franny.

She watches me manipulate the egg drippings onto the paper sack. She's not at all critical, just observing, and her easy acceptance makes me feel like staying close to her. I ask her about Berkeley, a place that for me is just a picture of stone throwing and people running from tear gas.

"It's pretty there. I live in a commune with some fairly interesting folks. I need a little distance, though. That's why I want work in San Francisco."

She's now chewing celery stalks spread with a tan goo.

"Sesame butter. Tastes like shit, but very healthy."

Mary wheels in a cart filled with Tabs, Frescas and coffee. We join the rest of the group who are listening to a dark-complexioned girl with long, black hair and a pixie face. She pauses until Mary leaves the room.

"If you ask me, he's just a very ordinary chauvinist pig. All that Other Reality bla-bla is straight out of twelfth grade cafeteria and we women sit in worshipful silence, listening to him, his spellbound Peanut Gallery. When he gets back here, I mean to ask him some straight questions, and I expect straight answers. If I don't get them, then I'm on my way."

I didn't talk about Zen Buddhism in grade twelve. Since they banned the Lord's Prayer in grade school, the closest we got to Other Reality was our math teacher giving us a few lessons in non-Euclidean geometry. It's true, a few of us visited a conference at the University of Toronto called Perception '67. It was supposed to be about altered states. We walked through a funhouse of tin foil, Smarties and Styrofoam and listened to a group called the "Fugs," but it was certainly not part of the high school curriculum.

Langley returns. He stands by the door in silence, willing us to quiet, to throw garbage in the wastebasket, to place our chairs in position and to sit. He leaves the door and places his chair on our level. He doesn't smile.

The dark girl raises her hand. He nods.

"This training is like my interview. I have no clearer idea

what this is all about than when I came in. In one morning you've managed to cover the entire history of the human race, as well as your own personal one, and not a word about the job. I want to know what this is leading to. I want to know why there are only women being trained here. If your main interest is a captive female audience, then I want to know that, so I can plan my time accordingly."

He smiles warmly into her dueling eyes.

"Thank you for sharing that with us, Janet."

He breaks contact with her and joins the rest of us. There is silence as we wait for Janet to make a decision. She undergoes an inward crumple and sinks into her seat.

"Okay, if there are no more comments at present we'll continue with the session."

He didn't fight her, but instead melted her, like Dorothy when she threw water on the witch. Those crease lines by his eyes that come from pain and smiling told her it was her choice, she could stay and be warmed or go outside to the cold.

It is clear to me that we've all just shared a further commitment: a closing of the circle, a tightening of the band. Langley's voice begins, and a slight wind caresses my face and moves down to tingle my spine. I catch his eye and know he has sent this air current as a probe. And I have felt it and reacted, letting him know I understand the dark places. He now recognizes the deepness of the magic in me, and we know that I have come to stay. His eyes move on, whispering secret messages to the next one. All this time he's also talking, sentences that are made for this world.

"Look, gang, I'm more than happy to tell you what we do here. Get the nuts and bolts part out of the way. We're a business. We sell educational materials, mainly through door-to-door sales, though we're expanding into other areas. You young women have been recruited to work in our children's branch – that is, your particular target population will be the mothers of young children. We use women for this population for the simple reason that our statistics show that women have the highest success rate in influencing these young mothers to take a greater interest in the pre-school development of their children."

He winks at Janet.

"You will, of course, all get a chance to familiarize yourselves with the merchandise itself. Let me assure you, it is very high-quality material. Since such a high level of interest has been expressed, Mary will now bring in some sample books and you can spend the rest of the afternoon familiarizing yourself with the product."

Mary wheels in a cart on which is a set of children's encyclopedias. She explains how the books have been organized, based on the latest findings in child development, to supplement and nurture the child's intellectual growth. Our suspicions are gently laid to rest.

Langley walks in as the sun begins to set and presents each of us with a dark-blue attaché case. Each of our names has been appliquéd in gold on the upper right corner. Inside is our sales kit, what we will present to customers. As we file out, he says good-bye to each of us by name.

Franny waits for me on the stairs.

"Do you think everybody will be back?"

"Sure," she smiles. "Who would miss a couple more days eye-fucking a hunk like that?"

We part ways and as the shadows lengthen, I dwarf myself. I've felt unique and special for most of the day, a forbidden occurrence in my recent life, so now it seems the lecture must begin.

You think that man cares about you? You think you've joined some group of outstanding human beings? You and your friends are a bunch of out-of-work, unskilled laborers about to be exploited by an entrepreneur who's only out to make a buck.

But he sees the magic in me, I try to protest.

What magic? You have no magic. There is no magic. You're an ugly, mean and stupid little girl, fooled by a con-artist who is laughing at you.

He's not real and you're not real either.

CHAPTER 5

*B*ranches on my window bang out the monotony of my death. Why can't I lie here not sleeping, and worry about big things, like napalmed children and rising food prices? Instead, I pass the night overwhelmed by petty loneliness: an empty food container with bits and pieces of somebody else's dinner caked on the sides, a blight on the earth, a living symbol of the failure of the socialist dream.

A key turns in the front door.

"Snow?"

Taye says it softly so as not to wake me.

I go into the living room. She seems smaller than the day she took me home with her. She stands in the soft hall light, struggling to remove her backpack. I help her.

"There's one guy who keeps calling. Talks through his nose."

"Ron. My ex-boyfriend. He'll ask you out soon, if he hasn't already."

She is much calmer than I remember her, like a tornado in its own eye.

"I'd love some tea. Would you be willing? . . . "

We go into the kitchen. She sits on a high stool by the counter and I search among the brightly colored packets in the drawer.

"Take the purple one. Jasmine."

I follow instructions.

"You look different." I focus on the kettle, avoiding GROWTH eye tactics.

"I'm much better. Centered. I'll show you something."

I hear her rummaging in her backpack and she returns with a sheaf of papers. We sip tea as she passes me one drawing after the other. Each is a hard-lined woman's head, open-scalped with things spilling out of it: snakes and dogs, vaginas and penises, books and lipsticks, bones and babies. I never learned how you're supposed to look at art. I concentrate desperately on trying to remember what the art teacher used to say when she liked something. Was it "Good try" or "Interesting direction"?

To my good fortune Taye doesn't seem to need a response.

"That's what was going on the day we met. I got it out in my drawings while I was camping with a friend up north. You ever been up north?"

"I come from up north, remember? And camping up north, where I come from, means summer camp in Muskoka with canoes, hot showers and C.A.R.E. packages from your parents."

She pauses, looking at me, realizing I'm trying to amuse her. Then her face breaks into a smile.

"I always thought where you come from was all wilderness full of folks in red woolen shirts and French accents looking for fur pelts."

"Though your ignorance of your northern neighbor's rapid industrial development is vast, I still give you credit for giving me a name that keeps me conscious of my Canadian heritage."

"You're okay, Snow. And I did feel bad walking out on you like that, after you'd just moved in."

I'm glad she feels guilty.

"It's only eleven. Come have a smoke with me. I've got the stuff in the other room."

It's so easy to agree. My parents' worst fears were true. They knew what I didn't: that my decision to try marijuana was made before I came to San Francisco. I knew that I'd smoke the same way I knew that I'd eat Chinese food and not go home a virgin. So what! I'll taste all the things the city is famous for.

It's funny how, just like the girl who descended the road to degradation in the *Evils of Marijuana* movie that we saw in assembly last year, I am succumbing to the malignant disease of peer pressure. I don't want Taye to think me naive and inexperienced, especially now when she seems ready to befriend me. There is no worse humiliation than to be judged by someone you admire and found to be wanting.

Like what happened in grade ten when Frieda called.

"Oh my," said my mother, totally insensitive to how high school status is defined, "she's been in bed for quite some time already. She'll call you tomorrow."

Listening from my room, I died a thousand deaths. Frieda was one of the in-crowd who had reached beyond the castle walls to make friends with me. Now, through my mother's astonished response at her "late" call, she would realize how immature and unworthy of her company I was.

Never again.

I follow Taye into the living room. She puts Simon and Garfunkel on the record player and from a hidden drawer under her loom takes a roller, papers and a cellophane bag.

"This loom was made especially for me. By a friend of the witch on the Amazon – actually it was one of her lovers. Why don't you get a candle? Same drawer as the tea."

I watch her roll the joint. She does it quickly, using a little machine, and then licks the paper. She lights up and takes a drag, doing it much more professionally than in the high school movie. When she waves for me to take it, I hold it between thumb and first finger, inhale a smallish amount and take a second breath to pull it down into my lungs. Controlling my impulse not to immediately cough out, I pass the joint back and Taye accepts without hesitation. My technique has fooled her. She believes me a woman of experience. Thank God for the *Evils of Marijuana* film.

We pass the cigarette back and forth, listening to the music. I think of Dustin Hoffman at that party at his parents' house in *The Graduate* and the lecture he got on the future of plastics. The lecturer's voice grows more vehement, his teeth turn into fangs.

"That's enough, eh?" I say.

She laughs. "Hey, now I'm sure you're from Canada."

Oh God, I'm caught. I haven't smoked enough and Taye has guessed that I'm really an innocent from the barren wastelands of North York.

"How'd you find out?"

"Elementary. I heard you say 'eh' at the end of a sentence. Anyone who does that is Canadian."

I breathe a sigh of relief. The flame on the candle is doing strange things.

"It's supposed to do that," says Taye. "It's called a strobe candle."

"Why?"

My mouth is suddenly very dry and it comes out funny.

"Why what?"

I can't remember what I asked. We watch the candle and listen to "Scarborough Fair."

The candle bursts into thousands of twinkling lights, just like two years ago at Expo '67 in Labyrinth. Then, there was a stunned silence, broken by a female New York voice screeching, "Oh my Gawd!"

This time Taye says, "You're probably wondering whether I'm homo- or heterosexual. I'm incurably hetero."

"Me too."

"But don't you sometimes wish you could get aroused by other women? You know, to be part of what's going on more, the movement I mean. And not to be dependent on them so much – I mean the men. I myself hate the dependence business more than anything else, the feeling that you can't do without someone. And then he feels you feeling that, and he gets scared and runs away because the last thing in the world he wants is a commitment and, for God's sake, to feel tied down or something. If I could choose to be with a woman, then I wouldn't have to be dependent on men. Understand?"

I nod.

"On the other hand, I can understand why the men are so wary. There's this passive, clingy type of woman who, while she attracts them, is eventually a very nauseating experience to be around. Not that I haven't met men like that too. No life of their own, just waiting to vampire it off somebody else. Well, at least women are getting out of that role. And thank God I finally broke it off with Ron."

I acknowledge that I know of whom she speaks.

"He's constantly calling, begging for me to let him cause a little more pain. I can't tell you how glad I am to be out of that relationship. No more just-not-to-be-lonely self-degrading compromises. Next time I will not settle for less than what I want."

We are both lying on our backs on the cushions. The candle is burning itself out, the record finished long ago.

"Snow, tell me you're not one of those frail, help-me-I'm-lost kind. I can't stand that type. They threaten my being. My group says I'm afraid of that side of myself."

She sits and lights another joint. Her eyes glisten, her long, dark hair falling over them as she concentrates not to burn her fingers.

"Coping skills. That's what's needed. Coping skills. I can only reach orgasm by external manipulation. And I talk a lot when I'm stoned. But I'm quite witty and intelligent, and also very good in bed. Besides, I have a right to an orgasm however I need to get it, right?"

"Yes."

"In my women's group I learned that everybody's responsible for their own actions. It's a good thing to know. I also have rape fantasies. I'm ashamed about it because I'm under no illusions what the real thing is like. From friends, you know. I guess the fantasies are a symptom of the deep, subconscious bind plaguing all women of our generation. Here we are, consciously knowing so much and inside terribly warped by the generations of experience we've inherited. Strength is so relative."

In the room there is silent darkness and inside my head windows with birds' wings fluttering outside them. Suddenly Langley peeks through the filmy curtains. I tell him to go away. Taye will not approve of our passive, female counterpoint at GROWTH. I search for a thought to share with her.

"I don't see men as strong as you do, Taye. To me most of them seem so frail and easily hurt."

Slowly she looks at me with such sadness, unshed tears and caring that it is frightening.

"That's the trap, Snow. You've fallen into the trap."

The moment between us is fragile, in touch with some Absolute Truth. There is no blame and no solution. She has made us classic victims. We are the napalmed children and for a precious moment I am absolved of guilt.

But just for a moment. Then I ask myself: Why don't you care more about the efficacy of Vitamin C and deodorant? Why does a conversation on a bus or in line at the supermarket seem beyond your capabilities? Will you ever have a home, a baby and a pediatrician?

"Goodnight, Taye. Got to get some rest so's I can get up bright and early and work towards next month's rent money."

Remorseful at my banality, I walk quickly towards my room.

"It's okay, Snow. Sleep well."

CHAPTER 6

Pete Seeger's "Little Boxes" is the most frightening song I know. Death hides in one of those boxes, inside an empty yogurt container on the Formica counter next to the refrigerator. And yet most women are trained to find this waiting for Death quite pleasant, comforted by the suds running through their fingers and the sound of squeaky-clean dishes afterwards.

"GROWTH," says Langley, "reaches out to the woman trapped in the complacency of her suburban home, surrounded by little children, feeling helpless in her dependency. Our program has been designed specifically to reach the housewives of the nation. They are perhaps the most neglected and exploited class of our day. We work with all ethnic sectors in the community – white, black, hispanic, you name it. Our target is the young mother, whatever her race, religion or color. Our goals are to facilitate her encounter with her own strength and to increase her ability to influence her children's future."

Sitting next to Franny I am bound to her within his spell, feeling connected and close. I am shy at the nakedness that must be showing in my eyes, but I know it's there in the others' too. I also know that Langley must be used to the adoration. But still he reacts with surprise and delight, as if for the first time, each time, with an innocence that sucks us like being pulled into quicksand.

He is framed today by colored charts, describing the different phases of our sales pitch, from the initial hello to the signing of the pay-by-installment contract. The reds and oranges of the charts make even warmer the brown of his eyes. Does he know this? Does it matter?

"By signing her name on the contract, by making this commitment without consulting her husband, the young mother is taking a giant step towards independence, to being her own woman. If our client is in the right income bracket, as was determined in our preliminary screening questions, she has made a decision against which there is no logical argument. There is no question that she has made a wise investment, and one she can afford. Her husband, if he objects, will be doing so only on the grounds that his male ego has been threatened, that his wife has taken a step without first obtaining his permission. By our client's insistence on her right to independent decision-making, she has gone that much further in realizing her potential. She is that much nearer to self-actualization."

He smiles and crinkles.

"And, of course, she and her entire family have acquired a lovely set of books."

I am so excited I have to remind myself to breathe. At last I may have found a way to be of use in the world, an opportunity to cause Good, a way to make my mark, contributing to society. As Langley has said, if I can influence one woman to see herself as exploited, help her take control of one part of her life, and move her towards independence, then she may influence her neighbor in the same way, and then maybe her cousin who has a cousin, and on and on until the world is a better place.

Despite all the doubts and despairs, there is a space deep inside me that still wants to believe in my magic; not to let Puff die. It's the kind of magic like in *The Last Unicorn*, the kind you can't predict or direct. Langley will teach me to plug into the source and be taken along in the majesty of the experience.

If my stomach would only calm down and stop bouncing back and forth through my rib cage. Am I on the edge of an abyss, or have I found an answer to all my searchings: a teacher, a mission and a way? Am I having a peak experience, or is this how it feels when you want sex with someone? Whatever happens, I need to protect myself from believing in dreams that can't come true.

Langley gives us a script to memorize. It begins with:

"Hi. I've been asked to call on mothers in the area. May I step in?"

Then you're supposed to step in. We take a break. Franny's having her doubts.

"I don't know whether I'm going to be any good at this. Despite all the romance, what we're doing is selling door-to-door. I just can't see myself trudging down those metal-mailboxed streets pushing on folks' doorbells. I'm too sensitive to rejection."

She makes a funny movement with her mouth, one side sliding down like a sad clown's face, asking me not to take her too seriously. But I do.

"I too prefer knocking on a door where I know they're glad to see me. But I think Langley's worked out this formula where just about anybody, if she follows the spiel and believes it will work, will end up selling. I also don't think he would have picked you, Franny, and spent the energy train-

56

ing you if he wasn't convinced you could do it. He's expecting a payoff from all this."

"You're not buying all that 'Romance of the Sword' business either, huh?"

"Of course not."

Franny's too realistic, a feet-on-the-ground type, to share my hallucinations.

"You look different today, Snow. Wha'd you do?"

"I'm breathing. No girdle and no bra. But it's a secret. Don't tell my mother. I'm hoping she won't notice the nipple outline."

Franny laughs and I'm warmed, glad we've changed the subject.

"I think that's the first time I've said the word 'mother' since I left home."

"When was that?"

"About a week ago. And you?"

"Beginning of last year, when I came to Berkeley to go to school. I'm supposed to go home, to Madison, next month. Only I have to lose thirty pounds first. I told them I had already lost it, and that was a big mistake."

I could talk about diets with her, but it's hard right now. Langley's words spin through my head, interrupting.

"Don't you feel that life is sometimes going by without you, Franny?"

"Cuz I'm fat you mean?"

She notices my distress.

"Oh, you mean existential crisis and all that. Life peaked when I was six years old, Snow. Then I was the darling of the entire family: blond curls and dimples, being begged for hugs and kisses. Then old Life went on to other people, I guess. I'd had my share."

"You're serious, aren't you, Franny? You don't look for any meaning anymore?"

"That's ridiculous. Of course I look for meaning. Being thin gives life meaning. Getting Langley into bed might give some meaning. I have an idea. The first one who gets him into bed gets a chocolate fudge sundae at Blum's. God, I'm clever. You see how I've built in an only-win situation?"

I can't help laughing.

"Franny, you're just like my counselor at camp who told me to quit worrying my head about world-shaking questions that can never be answered and get myself a boy-friend. She said I'd feel much better."

"Was she right?"

"I guess so. When I got a boyfriend, I stopped thinking."

We giggle together, but it leaves me empty. I'm glad when Langley calls us back. He's propped a huge drawing on an easel, labeled "The Flow Chart of Life." At the top, printed in capitals, is the word God.

"Don't get uneasy, kids," says Langley. "We won't start preaching at you. The word God is a metaphor. Call it Destiny, or Life Force, or the Instinct to Survive, or Energy, or the Will of the People, or Respect for Human Dignity. It's however you personally define what it's all about. It's what you're willing to put yourself on the line for. Now, let yourself flow into the flow chart, and I'll explain how it works."

Again his voice takes on the deep hypnotic quality, sentences not logical, words no longer matter.

The colored lines and arrows of the chart move downwards from God to join more complex masses of triangles, circles and squares. There are captions, not all of them in English, but also Chinese, Hebrew and Arabic and some hieroglyphs that are totally unrecognizable. Langley quotes poetry, Hindu and Japanese, talks about Permanency and Impermanency, and somehow it all connects. Mandalas emerge and draw my body forward, out of its skin, into the chart itself. I myself am in the flow and discover the lines joining things are not simple dot-to-dot connections but tiny air-tight test tubes filled with amniotic fluid. I push my way from tube to tube, down the birth canal, pausing sometimes for guidance, until I spill forth into the mouth of a giant mother whale. Not frightened, I move, Pinocchio style, to her stomach, and then in one regurgitating tidal wave she pulls me back, out and up through her spouting hole, to God.

After the crystal clarity of joining, I am to be recycled as a fish. Next plunge I will no longer need the test tube. Now at home in regular water, I will let it protect and buoy me. Not resisting, I will let it pulse against and through my skin, and my mind will ooze out, keeping the electric balances in order. It is good to be part of. The others in here with me feel it too, and let their heads ooze into mine, and mine into theirs, and together we feel the bouncing of the planets.

"So you see," Langley's voice returns, "our approach to you, and you to your clients, is a manifestation of a philosophical approach to life. Life is Good. Life is Meaningful. Life is an invitation to activity, to creativity, to procreativity. Believing. Beliving. Begrowing. The Way is what's important. Read Camus. Read the Tao. Each Step. Each Task. To perfect and move on. Your approach to each step of the demonstration needs to be in keeping with this spirit of dedication and care. The minutest detail is deserving of attention and love. As if you were exploring a lover's body."

This time I know he's looking only at me.

"We'll stop for lunch now. Afterwards you'll meet your group trainers who will be with you throughout your entire association with GROWTH. We'll take a few minutes for questions."

"Wow," whispers Franny, "what did they put in the Kool Aid?"

The flow chart is ironing itself back into lines and squares and circles. Teetering on the edge of a not-entirely-unknown plane, I doubt what's been.

"Yes, Snow," says Langley.

"What if some of us are not very fast swimmers?"

"You were once. It's just a matter of relearning, Snow. And anytime you need me I'll be here."

My father taught me to swim. I remember the smell of the chlorine at the Bloor Street Y, where I lost my silver ring with the three turquoise stones that they had given me, and how my father held his hands just beneath me while I floated.

"If there are no more questions, we can call the formal theoretical part of your training over. Informally, we will continue as long as you are with us. But remember, theory without results is not GROWTH's way. Here Life is to be lived and not just talked about. Here at GROWTH, that means going out into the field and bringing back results. Results here mean sales, and the sense of power and awareness when you make them. Good luck, kids. And have a nice lunch. You deserve it."

We eat a silent meal, each alone with her experience.

Franny, Sarah, Janet and I follow Elaine, our trainer. She is an American advertisement for freshness and health: Hi there, welcome to the big country, pull up a chair and sit down. . . . I have to distance her life, that is a simple, straight road, from my spirals and spheres in order to listen to her. I switch to good-student mode and absorb information.

"This afternoon we are going to learn the scripted text that accompanies the presentation of the materials you received in your kit. But we are not going to just learn the words. We are going to work on something called 'delivery,' the way you say it. You will learn to *clear* your presentation of emotional implication. Emotion, your personal feelings and needs, is put aside and the words are passed on cleanly, as information. Your receiver, the one listening, is allowed absolute space for her own personal processing and emotional responses. You do not manipulate. You do not try to control. You merely state your information and allow total freedom of response."

She turns to Franny.

"Repeat after me: Hi. I've been asked to call on mothers in the area. May I step in?"

"Hi . . ."

"No. Stop right there. No smiling. No emotional input. Just the words, please."

"Hi . . ."

"You said it with a question in it. Again, please."

Franny's eyes shine with hope, like at the start of a new diet.

CHAPTER 7

A letter from home, air mailed straight from the movie about the blob that came from outer space. Initially a harmless substance, it started to grow, until it threatened to take over the world. But the innocent-looking blue aerogram doesn't fool me. The choice of aerograms over envelope already indicates membership in the international plot to suppress individualism. I get pleasant satisfaction in ripping it open on the undotted line.

However, I am not fully prepared for the attack. It is filled with words like "thoughtless", "childish" and "self-destructive." I had thought there might also be a little "Hi, how are you?"

It's not that I don't understand her thinking. My mother was taught that to do anything for herself, without taking everyone else's welfare into account first, was the worst of sins. For her there is no such thing as wanting, in a personal sense. Your acts are either for or against another. Therefore, my leaving home is an aggressive act against her and merits retribution.

Accepting the conceptual base, her logic is faultless. But

my mind is overtaken by the invading blob, logic and understanding are forgotten, and all light is blocked out. Pus swells in my veins. Childhood purple rages threaten to overwhelm and suffocate me. I become the vat of poison that I think she sees. After all, she does know me better than anyone else does. Running on hate-filled energy, my purpose is to use and destroy. Did her life end when mine began?

I throw the letter in the garbage and call Ernie. A machine, born from the same sad head that invented the aerogram, answers. I pray that I will never live to see the day when I will use phone machines and aerograms, that I will fight to preserve one spark of humanity from the rampant onslaught of technology.

Alone, after the shelling, I nurse my wounds. Why can't I just accept myself for who I am, as slightly less than mediocre, and get on with doing whatever everybody else is doing?

Still, there is that sense of something more and better and beyond. Langley sees it in me and his knowing may mean that out there in the real world there are others who know about planets and orbits and star-crossed happenings. Maybe there is still a chance that I can live outside of books and movies. Maybe there are others who understand the connection between phone machines and Vietnam.

The phone rings. I answer, defiantly human.

"Is Taye there? Probably not, huh."

"No, Ron. She's not."

"You okay, Snow? You sound like you're kind of angry."

"How did you guess?"

"Talk to me a little. There's no reason for you and me not to get along."

"I suppose not."

"Listen, I'm not saying that a lot of the things Taye must

have told you about me aren't accurate. But there are two sides to a story. Why don't I come over and meet you?"

"Is this how you come on with all the Snows?"

"Not all. But Taye has a good intuitive sense about people. I usually like the people she likes. She hasn't said I'm violent or anything, has she?"

"No, it's not that. I feel like I'm doing something behind her back. Even talking to you. Let me talk to her first."

"Where you from, Snow?"

I tell him.

"That explains it. Canadian Snow. Heavier, longer to thaw."

I hang up and contemplate abandoning all forms of communication, until the phone rings again. It's Ernie's gentle voice.

"I was in the shower. Just got your message, little one. How are you keeping?"

"Not so good. But I thought it might help to see you."

"A delightful idea. I'll take you to the park. Be ready in half an hour and I'll be at your doorstep."

And thus it will end: the touch of a cold knife, abandoned to die in Golden Gate Park, left rotting until the smell and circling insects attract attention. I'm not crazy. R.D. Laing says not to be paranoid in these days is to be crazy. I am going out with a sexual pervert, consciously inviting destruction.

What should I wear to my death? Jeans, sweater and no bra. My bralessness will comfort my mother, knowing I gave reasonable cause for my murder. This is my last unselfish act before dying.

We take the bus from the city center and leave the slick mannequin toothpaste commercial people that live there, moving into more residential areas. It is early enough in the day that the fog hasn't rolled in and the sky outside sparkles.

64

The bus fills with folks with shopping bags and kids and Kleenex. The familiarity of the scene is both a comfort and a threat. A few glance at Ernie's eye makeup, but most don't notice. Ernie, reading a James Bond book, doesn't care.

As we near the park the bus people begin to change character. They are dressed like the hippies I've seen on the news: loose clothes, bright colors and beads. Most, including the children, are barefoot.

I watch the girls, seeing, for the first time, breasts in public. It's not like seeing girls changing clothes together, shy and quick to cover. Here, there is neither coyness nor boldness. The girls and their families treat breasts as part of the body, connected with the rest. Seeing them through the India gauze blouses or outlined against T-shirts, I watch small and large ones sway with the rhythm of the bus. My own, unused to freedom, move more self-consciously. Ernie catches me watching and smiles.

We reach the park and he takes my hand.

"We'll take a rapid stroll through some of the main thoroughfares and then I'll take you to the Japanese Tea Garden, where you'll see the tourists and join me in a cup of tea."

"Do I look okay? I don't stick out too much from the rest?"

My words sound strange to me, out of place, after the silence of the bus ride.

"Don't worry, smallface. I'll take you to the flea market one day soon and we'll dress you like you should be. There's definitely been an improvement since Macy's, though."

We enter the park. It has no boundaries: absolute, limitless space. I hold Ernie's hand a little tighter.

"I saw you looking at those girls in the bus. Are you perhaps, like me, an F-A-G?"

"I don't think so."

"Ah. In the process of discovery, are we?"

"No, not really. To tell you the truth, I'm totally lacking in experience."

"How precious. You really are a special find, aren't you?"

"Ernie, I'm pretty sure I like men, though."

"Well, so do I, love. I won't hold it against you."

This may be the first conversation in my life where I'm not planning what to say. I have no expectations with him, no tension. I can say or not say, and he will keep holding my hand.

"Ernie, you want to teach me to be your friend?"

He stops walking, and tilting my face up into his, just looks. He is on the verge of sorrow, eyes softening and deepening. He makes a tiny sound, a soft intake of breath, and then starts us walking again. I try to take in the park.

The people about us are strolling or sitting on the grass, playing flutes and backgammon and throwing frisbees. The smell of marijuana is in the air. Children, most of the smallest ones naked, bounce back and forth among groupings of adults, making it impossible to sort out who belongs to whom. Their little bodies have a soft sweetness, brushing against each other, with an instinct not to cause harm. Again I'm caught by the eyes of a Negro man as I smile at children. This one has long hair in thousands of braids, and wears a black leather vest over bare skin. Before I can panic, he smiles back, and then looks away, the interaction completed. A smile from a stranger, a moment of absolute naked intimacy, received, acknowledged and closed. His black skin continues to reverberate against the green of the park.

"Something's starting over there."

Trembling, I follow Ernie towards a gathering crowd.

In the center is a guy with long, curly hair and wire-rimmed glasses, juggling colored balls. He has a sweet smile as he concentrates on keeping his six balls in the air. He and six others, scattered around the perimeter, wear uniforms of leotards, jeans and suspenders, their faces made up in red, white and blue paint. The others place colored boxes around the juggler.

"Who are they?"

"They're from across the bay. Very good – I've seen them before."

Their boxes in place, the six jangle tambourines and perform acrobatics: somersaults, flips in the air and other incredible feats. The crowd around me grows bigger, with no pushing, as people settle into place, giving the smaller ones room at the front. A giant guy in front of me, tattoos running up and down his arms, asks if it's difficult for me to see. We change places and I sit down in time to receive a jug of wine being passed from hand-to-hand, mouth-to-mouth. A little girl climbs into my lap.

The juggler finishes with a flourish, picks up a guitar and settles on a low red box. He plays a few notes and the others gradually slow their motions, until he strums a loud chord and they freeze.

"We are going to tell you a story about a little girl named Angela and how one day she fell down a hole. At the end of the hole was a land full of strange creatures, most of whom she couldn't understand. Actually, they couldn't much understand her either. But not to worry." He strums the guitar and flashes his sweet smile. "Everything turns out fine in the end."

Ernie asks me in a whisper if I've heard about Angela Davis.

"She's a Negro Communist teacher who got fired from Berkeley, right?"

I recite the answer, proud that I know. And I almost forgive my mother her letter, in gratitude for my political education.

He laughs. "Watch the show."

Through songs, acting and mime, the seven performers tell the story of Angela, a little girl who meets the characters in the Alice book, all of them also with political identities. She shrinks or grows tall depending on whom she's talking to, on how much they harass or support her, and she keeps trying to answer questions that don't make sense.

The troupe plays all the characters, transforming the Hare into the Cat into the Doormouse. I laugh along with the crowd at their peculiarities and inability to understand little Angela's logical train of thought. But the Queen orders her head cut off and the little girl in my lap is frightened. I hold her tight as Angela climbs on the tallest box, looks around and with a very believable air of sudden enlightenment, laughs and calls out the familiar, "You're nothing but a pack of cards." The Queen and her attendants wither away. The crowd claps and whistles. My little girl cheers.

But the guitar player calls for quiet.

"Hey, folks, we're not a nationally endowed institution. Your loud applause is not enough. We will continue to bring you people's entertainment at people's prices, meaning whatever you can afford, as long as you help to support us. So, folks, as we pass the hat, show us your warm appreciation."

He starts to play and sing as the others go through the crowd. The song has a simple tune and repeats:

They can take our park
They can try and bring on the dark
But evil brings on its own destruction.

We can stop their war
We can remember who we are
And together bring our own construction.

I sing too and the little girl gets up from my lap and dances towards a woman in a long dress who reaches out to catch her. A hat with some change and a couple of marijuana cigarettes is passed to me. I put in a dollar and Ernie pulls me to my feet.

"Now the teahouse."

We sit under cherry blossoms, next to curved bridges. Ernie orders rosehip tea for himself, for the Vitamin C he says, and Darjeeling for me, for the mystery.

"So, is it a little better now?"

"Ernie, you can see it's better. But it's hard for me to talk about it. I've felt things I've never felt before in my life. I was down about a letter from my mother and then that little girl sits in my lap. I've never had a child sit in my lap before. Watching that show, while I was holding her, it all seemed to mean more. Do you understand?"

"I think so. It's like when I'm in a relationship, a good one I mean, I feel more about everything. It makes me more generous. Like now. You wouldn't have gotten me out here if I wasn't involved with somebody. When I'm not, I retreat into a black cloud and sulk."

I nod to let him know he has understood. The tea comes and we sip silently. The wind plays with the cherry blossoms and the couple next to us wonders if they can pay with traveler's checks.

"The political people I've known have been pretty pretentious, lecturing all the time. That group today was laughing. They made me laugh too."

"Sure. It's nice when they don't yell and harangue. There's enough hate and anger around, enough anti-life people. I've been exposed to my share of them, humiliated and hurt by them, until I was so mad myself that I started to froth back."

He looks to see if he's scared me. I hold his eyes and

surprise myself in no fear. A tear runs down my cheek and I look away. Ernie brushes it off.

"Don't despair, Snow. It's the Age of Aquarius and love will conquer all."

"Yeah, after the revolution."

"Now you're catching on."

With the fog in thick and the air turning cooler, we move towards the bus stop. The park empties with us and I can hear our footsteps on the concrete walk. There are so many questions I'd like to ask him, like what does he do for a living, how old is he, where does he come from, if he was ever heterosexual and what does he really think about me. But all the information seems too mundane. Ethel Rosenberg wouldn't have asked silly questions like that.

CHAPTER 8

I read Taye's copy of *The Teachings of Don Juan*. I too want a safe place and a teacher to guide me out of my body and into the air. I need to be taught the signs of danger, how to go through them without being damaged, and how to come home again. Taye had her witch on the Amazon. It seems only fair that I should have a guide too. Does it define me as a weak and dependent personality that I want to be scooped up and trained to be more than I am?

I already know I can't be like most people. I am resigning myself to the fact that I don't care about the things they do: like body odor or having a profession or even baby skulls bashed against a wall in a time before I was born. In their eyes I'm sure I deserve to have died in an oven.

Then again, maybe I did. And was born again.

I do know some things that they don't know. I know what it is to leave my body and fly, though I never thought of it as anything special until reading Taye's book. I did it all the time as a little kid, high over my backyard, spying on my parents and their friends. I flew over mountains too, the cold air sometimes tickling my body left behind, and into oceans filled with fish and sea serpents. But like the tea parties with Grace, or the interludes in the jungle with Free, I never mentioned my flying to people. I didn't want to be locked up in a loony bin. And so I never found a teacher.

I'm stuck in a world that doesn't suit me; never to be a heroine, never to fight a dragon, never to outwit a witch. I am left here to suck off the living material around me, a bloated parasite, weakening the Life Force of anyone who comes close, a cancerous contagious amoeba who enters the bloodstream of the host organism and poisons from within. It's a shame I can't trade in this world in exchange for another.

And yet perhaps there's hope. Perhaps in Langley I've finally found a teacher. It's difficult, however, to reconcile his wisdom with the mercenary training that I get from Elaine.

We are completing the sales course, working on details of how to hand the pen to our customer so she will automatically take it and then sign the contract for the thirty-six installment payments. The method is as follows: Do not look at her as you hand her the pen, but concentrate only on the dotted line where her signature needs to go. As you concentrate on that line, say: "And you sign right here." At the same time, you see her name already there. With total concentration keep staring at the line and seeing her name, until her hand moves and the name appears for real.

The entire sales script is constructed this way. The customer's responses are known before she gives them. Her answers – for example: "Of course my children's education is important to me" – are included as part of the text we've been given. If at any point she doesn't give the prepared answer, this is a sign she is not going to commit at the end. If this occurs, you are to pack up as quickly as possible and move on to the next house to try again.

"In life," says Elaine, "the moment you realize you're going in the wrong direction, cut your losses and get on another road."

"It seems sort of Machiavellian to me," I tell Franny at coffee break. "You're with someone as long as he's useful to you and then forget it. Maybe there are some interesting sidetracks off that main road."

"Come on, Snow. Don't get overdramatic. Elaine just means it as a little common folk wisdom, like don't throw good money after bad, or stop beating a dead horse. You're just out there to sell encyclopedias. Keep that in mind."

"Something doesn't feel right."

Franny's high on the new diet. She sounds like Elaine when she answers.

"I know what it is too. You're afraid of your own power. You know you can influence people. You know you can go out there and get what you want and you're scared of it. It's a combination of passivity and lack of confidence, just like those women you'll be selling to. We're not out there to have a neighborly chat. We're there to give them a chance, maybe for the first time in their lives, to make an independent decision. Don't be a chicken shit, Snow."

"Franny, you've become a convert, haven't you?"

"If I'm coming on too strong, I'm sorry. I liked it better too when we were sitting around getting eye-fucked. But like the lady said, we live in the world and nothing comes for free. So we'll make a few bucks at this, I'll lose a few pounds and we'll all go on living. And one day, if I'm a good girl, Mick Jagger will invite me home for the weekend. In other words, what've we got to lose?"

We walk into the office for our first official morning meeting with the entire staff.

Laurie hands us pink beanies and points us into the small auditorium. The room is filled with about fifty women, all in

73

colored hats: trainees are in pink, Elaine and the other trainers wear dark purple, the other women wear green, red or
blue. I notice that no one seems to be over thirty.

As my watch hand touches eight, Mary, in a pure-white
beanie, walks to the mike. She wills the room to quiet;
standing still, pulsating her electric current around our
chairs. I want to ask Franny if she thinks they've wired the
beanies, but I'm unable to open my mouth.

"Good morning, seekers."

"Good morning, Mary," they answer.

"One, two, three," she says, and they all sing.

> Out we go to the streets,
> Ready for today's destiny,
> To know what we will meet
> Unraveling life's surprises.
>
> Keep your head cool
> There are no rules
> You are beauuuuutiful.
>
> Out we go to the streets,
> Searching for useful answers.
> Just around the next bend
> Dreams unfulfilled may be waiting.
>
> Keep your head cool
> There are no rules
> You are beauuuuutiful.
>
> Out we go to the streets
> Stretching our own potential
> Power is the result
> That belief brings to the searching.
>
> Keep your head cool
> There are no rules
> You are beauuuuutiful.

There is silence as the song leaves the room.

"For the benefit of you trainees, that was the 'Seekers' Song.' We sing it every morning, and by tomorrow I'm sure you'll be joining in with us."

It all sounds like camp. I like camp.

"Trainees, at the end of the meeting your car boss, in a dark-blue beanie, will call your name. I wish you a rewarding day as you accompany her in the field, and look forward to hearing your reports after you've watched the process in action."

Whispers of a new current tickle the back of my neck.

"Ah, yes," says Mary. "Here's Langley."

In a powder-blue, open-necked shirt and loose gray pants with a pleat at the waist, he walks casually down the center aisle to the microphone. The only male in the organization, surrounded by groomed and eager-to-please women, he takes his monarchial position on the dais and looks right at me.

"So, Snow. You're thinking I've got one helluva set-up here, aren't you?"

Laughing, they follow his eyes to look at me, turning shades of red. I focus on the laces of my new Roots shoes.

"Hey, Snow, don't be shy. You're absolutely right. I do have one helluva set-up here, and I'm proud of it. You can lift up your head and start feeling proud to be part of us. I'm talking to all of you new trainees. Glad to have you on board."

He crinkles and twinkles and I can't help but crinkle and twinkle back.

Franny sighs beside me.

"Now, who has an achievement story for us this morning?"

A small woman with very red curly hair under her green beanie raises her hand.

"Yes, Barbara. I encourage and support you in your decision to take part this morning."

Barbara's voice, through the microphone, bounces from the ceiling, each word significant through the amplification.

"I've always wanted a leather coat, ever since I was little. And my parents always said it was a waste of money. They said a girl doesn't need a leather coat, that she doesn't wear it out, like a boy does. A leather coat for a girl makes no sense. And I grew up believing that a leather coat for me was a waste. I always found more important things to spend my money on."

I look around the room and each one is hanging on Barbara's every word.

"Then, last Friday, something happened. I woke up and decided that girls deserve leather coats."

They all giggle.

"As soon as I went out, I discovered that right behind my building, all the time, was a leather shop, with the blue leather coat of my dreams."

There's a lot of laughter now and a few start clapping, Langley among them.

"So, of course, I bought it."

She smiles broadly, turns for a nod from Langley, who says, "Now, all together . . . "

They chant.

"To know what I want is to find what I want is to get what I want."

"Thank you, Barbara. Very well done."

Langley puts his arm around her shoulders and gives her a little hug.

"All right, everybody. Ready for Destiny."

They suddenly slump in their chairs, stretched out, uncrossed feet in front of them, their hands limp at their sides.

76

Closing their eyes, they slowly exhale as their heads loll onto their chests. Langley watches quietly as they go through these preparations. I peek out from sideways eyes and am glad to catch Franny looking puzzled and a little scared.

Langley begins to speak in an even lower and sexier voice than normal.

"Today is July 18, 1969. This we know."

"Today is July 18, 1969. This we know." They chant back.

"This we know."

"This we know."

"You will meet your Connect today. This we know."

"This we know."

"She is a young mother. This we know."

"This we know."

"She is alone at home with her small children. This we know."

"This we know."

"She has hair the color of . . . of chocolate cake. This we know."

"This we know."

Langley's eyes are closed too.

"Our Connect's eyes are sad, with a hint of searching in them. She is dressed in, is it a pattern? Yes, a patterned blouse in soft blues. This we know."

"This we know."

He's swaying slightly, back and forth.

"Her living room is messy with kids' toys and unfinished breakfast meals, but it is recent clutter and otherwise cared for and warm. The corduroy couch where you are sitting together is frayed but comfortable to your body. She smiles at you shyly. This much we know."

Barely audible they answer, "This much we know."

There is now a long pause. The only sound is the in-sync

breathing. One of the trainees starts to giggle and turns it into a cough. My own breathing has slowed down incredibly and I feel relaxed, like in a tub of hot water. I let my eyes close for a little, until I hear Langley's voice start again.

"This we know."

"This we know," I too whisper.

"I am at Cause."

"I am at Cause."

They open their eyes and stretch like cats.

"Trainees, we know that since you've been at GROWTH you've been feeling a little strange, seeing and feeling things that your former life did not allow."

The old-timers giggle again, at our expense.

"Just let yourselves go with it. Keep your relaxed feeling, and have a successful day in the field. At the end of the closing song you will meet your car boss, who will look after you in the field. Tomorrow morning we will meet again here. Now Mary will lead us in our Energy Escalator song."

The mood changes again, this time to the beat of a Sousa march.

> This is my oath
> I come from GROWTH.
> To win the game
> Just sign your name.
> To free the ropes
> We must have hopes.
> Ya, ya, ya!

Bridget, my car boss, calls me. With no time to organize thoughts and perceptions, I grab my jacket and briefcase, toss my beanie to Laurie who collects them, and follow Bridget and three others outside, up and behind GROWTH offices, to her car.

CHAPTER 9

I run after Bridget through a place called Daly City, jumping over hedges, avoiding snarling dogs, pretending not to notice suspicious faces peeking from behind closed curtains. Sometimes sad and lonely women, clawed by sticky fingers, open their doors, releasing the noise of blaring televisions. And mostly repelled by the "Hi, I've been asked to call on mothers in the neighborhood," they shut themselves in again, in fear. One day the faces are all black, but the responses are the same.

We do get inside a house two or three times a day and at least one of these entrances finishes with a sale. The first day, Bridget sells to the woman Langley described in the morning meeting. She whispers "Bingo" to me as we both recognize her brown hair and patterned blouse. I'm not surprised to see her. Once inside her messy but comfortable living room, I sit in a corner and watch Bridget go through her paces.

Each of the following mornings Langley describes the "Connect" and Bridget finds her during the day. On the third day out our Connect is a tall dark person with permanent furrows in her forehead. She listens attentively to

Bridget, but absolutely refuses to sign the contract. Bridget feels terrible and when we get back to the office, asks for a private session with Langley.

Each night, at home with sore legs, despite my Roots shoes, I have barely enough energy to crawl into bed and set my clock. Exhausted as I am, I don't sleep well. New nightmares have started to plague me. Ordered rows of SS officers repeat the same endless movement: right arms crooked at the elbow, raised to chest, then flung out straight in front of them. Elaine, Bridget, Franny and I are among the uniformed troops. In the morning, when I see Langley, the dark uniforms are banished and I feel light again.

Friday evening I call home.

"Hello," says my mother's voice going cold as ice on recognizing me. "Is there something you wanted?"

"Just to say hi."

There is no response.

"Did you get my letter?"

"Yes. Do you want me to do anything about your university applications?"

"Just the one for York. Send that one, okay?"

I can feel her ice seeping into my bones.

"That one's already been sent. Are you planning to give me your phone number?"

"No." I try to make my voice soft. "I need this privacy right now, Mom. I wish you would understand."

"You have the heart of a snake. Your father wants to talk to you."

"Did you hear what she said to me?"

He keeps his own voice calm.

"You've hurt her very badly, you know. She really does love you. We both do. I wish you could be friends."

"So do I, Dad."

"Sweetie, why don't you come home now? We'll go up to

80

the cottage like usual. Spend some time together. I'm worried about you out there."

"I'm absolutely fine, Dad. That's what I'm calling to tell you. Like I wrote, I'm working. And tonight I'm going out with a friend of my roommate's. And the weather is great and I've been to Golden Gate Park . . . "

My voice trails off as I feel him not listening.

"Why don't you come out here and visit, Dad?"

He laughs.

"Honey, you do what's best for you. When you get back we'll have a good long talk. It's been too long since that happened. Your mother's been telling me that and she's right. Now don't spend any more of your money, and next time, call collect."

There's a pause while he talks to her in the background.

"Mother wants to know if she should mail your trench coat."

"That would be nice. Good-bye, Daddy. And say good-bye to Mom for me. Write."

"You are a self-destructive person, Snow," says Taye. "Calling your parents is self-destructive. Going out with Ron is self-destructive. He's a user. He'll eat you up and spit you out. He sucked me dry."

"Are you sure you feel okay about my seeing him?"

"Absolutely. It's just that I like you and I don't want to see you hurt. As for myself, watching him with others is clinically interesting. Actually, right now I'm playing my regular role in this whole drama. I give dire warnings, you go off anyway and I sit and wait for the predicted and predictable outcome and feel righteous about it."

She pats me on the cheek as she goes to her room.

"Snow, I think I might soon decide to introduce you to some of the heretofore unexplained mysteries of life. My group, I mean. That is if you want to."

"Sure, Taye. Whenever."

I begin the complicated procedure of getting dressed for my date. I can't wear something that's too sexy because that would project that I want to go to bed with him, and then, I'm either obligated or a prick tease. On the other hand, I can't purposely look like a hag and spend the evening watching him watching his watch.

I'm tempted to call Ernie for advice, but stick to my decision not to be in touch unless he calls me. I keep a very delicate balance in my head of who owes who what. Ernie gave me a lot that day he took me to the park; I can't ask for more. It's a "saving-face" procedure. I measure, by the density of their spider-like feelers, shadings of others' energies: twisting, bending, reaching out, gathering in, beckoning, rejecting, or maintaining a holding pattern. And thus I gear my own energy output accordingly.

I decide myself on what to wear: jeans, a blouse and a sweater. This way I don't have to wear a bra and yet can count on the double layer to obscure nipple outline. I put on light makeup, eyes and lips, and brush my hair hard until it curls slightly at the shoulders. I choose shoes with small heels, making sure not to tower over Ron. The image in the mirror reflects the proper degree of acceptability without overt arousal. The doorbell rings.

"Hey, Taye." It's the nasal voice.

"Snow, Ron's here," she yells from her room.

"Taye, you can come out here and say hello to me."

I wait a few minutes in my room to avoid their uncomfortable reunion. When I do go out, they're hugging each other.

"Whoops!"

Taye laughs and doesn't move away from this medium-height, well-built guy with long, sandy-colored hair, full beard and glasses.

Ron turns his head to look at me. "So you're Snow."

"Good guess."

They move away from each other and I stand by my bedroom door where I'm rooted in place.

"Snow comes from Toronto," says Taye. "Hopelessly middle class, but with potential. Sense of humor, guts, open to improvement. A little on the clutchy side, but she's aware of it. Altogether, she's on a fairly high level of consciousness, perhaps as a result of having grown up in an igloo."

Ron looks uncomfortable, but smiles. I don't.

"Hey, Taye, Ron. I have the feeling that you two might enjoy having this evening together. I'll just make my way back to my room here and a good book, okay? Nice to have met you, Ron."

I start the turn for my exit.

"Snow, let me at least finish the introductions. Ron lives in Marin County, in the bosom of the last word in liberated communities. He himself is the epitome of non-chauvinist, non-possessive, you-have-your-orgasm-first-dear masculinity. He is, however, a little short on the commitment and responsibility side. He is extremely creative and I think you two will be very good for each other. So it's me that's going to my room to read a book, and I hope you two have a lovely time."

She leaves before anybody can stop her.

"You mustn't mind us," he says. "Taye and I are very old friends. We're used to each other's routines."

He leans back against the wall, fiddling with his car keys. I like that he doesn't try to make conversation.

"Let's go," I say.

Ron breathes a sigh of relief and puts out his hand. We ride in a brown Volkswagen with orange flowers painted on it.

"Where are we going?"

"Not too far. To a coffee house that I like. 'The Grateful Dead' are rehearsing something there and it'll be a very creative, hip, liberated evening."

He smiles and glances over.

"And because I have a retarded level of consciousness, I don't know who 'The Grateful Dead' are. So I guess Taye was right about both of us, eh?"

"She usually is. I told you she's extremely intuitive."

Ron concentrates on driving and I try to figure out how I feel about him. Physically he's not my type; too solid inside his body, too compressed. He takes out a cigarette and offers me one. I turn him down and feel comfortable; in charge, like I did on dates in Toronto. Ron is not a potential danger for me. He doesn't attract and he doesn't threaten. He's as harmless as Ernie, though not as interesting. But he caused Taye to feel both pain and wanting. No wonder he's not ready to give her up.

The coffee place is medium-sized. We thread our way through smoke and tables to chairs wedged between others. Ron brings cafe con leche and carrot cake from the self-service bar. The band is playing. I can't understand the words and the music bangs against my head. Everybody else, including Ron, is jumping. I'm the only one who can't get into it. The others are in costumes: Indian headdresses, stovepipe hats, cloaks and robes, and they kiss and hug and vibrate to the music. People call "hi" to Ron and he waves back. The smell of marijuana is making me whoozy and I feel like quietly slipping away. I fight a headache and try to smile when he looks at me, waiting to be taken home.

Then suddenly the world ends. I'm inside a huge stomach cramp, manipulated by a giant, pulsating muscle. Gravity's gone and I drip off the edge of my chair like a watch in a Salvador Dali painting. Time is suspended in a silent black hole between things.

One, two, three seconds. And then the projector in the sky starts again. There is an explosion of laughter and I realize that whatever it was, we all went through it together. Ron is looking at me and laughing hard.

"What the hell is so funny?"

He laughs and laughs.

"You should see yourself, Snow. You were looking so uptight and aloof before. Now you're just a quivering bunch of nerves."

He finally controls his giggles.

"That was what's called an earthquake. About a three, I'd say, on the Richter. Welcome to San Francisco."

I begin to cry and he puts his arm around me. The music starts again and I rest on his chest, sniffling. Eventually he asks if I'm ready to go.

"I'll take you to my house in Stinson and bring you back to Taye's tomorrow."

I don't argue.

His house is a cottage in the garden of a bigger house: three small rooms and lots of wood. It smells like cats. I sit on a cushion in the living room, with a glass of red wine, listening to Joni Mitchell.

"Special for you," he says.

He sits beside me and takes my hand.

"Tired? I'll try and wake you up a little," and he kisses me while pulling me down to lie beside him.

I tense and then will myself to let go. He's not an ugly man. This is the plan and best to get it over with, as fast as possible. No attraction, no threat; in a few minutes I will be an experienced woman.

"Let's move to the bed," I say.

He's up and leading me by the hand. Without looking at Ron, I get undressed as fast as I can and slip under the slightly grungy sheets. I ask him to turn out the light. His naked body touches me and I try to imagine my math teacher. His fingers play with my breasts and then move down to the clitoris. It's not a bad feeling, but he goes on tweaking and rubbing until it gets uncomfortable. I realize he won't stop until I've had some meaningful experience, so I make a few sounds and move around a little. He puts his penis inside.

At first, it hurts. Then it changes to an irritating pressure, like a tongue depressor. After a few minutes, there's a little ripping feeling, like peeling off a scab. Then his thing kind of pulses inside and he collapses on top of me. I push him off gently. My thighs are sticky.

"You want me to get you a towel or something?"

"That would be nice."

He hands me a towel and I put it under the covers and wipe around. He's turned on the bedside lamp so we both can see the bloodstains on the towel when I pull it out.

"Hey, you're having your period. Far out."

"No. It's not that. I was a virgin."

"You're really a laugh, Snow. A virgin, sure. You know, I like you. Now let's get some sleep."

I move to the edge of the bed, my back to him, and curl in a ball; mission accomplished.

CHAPTER 10

*I*n the morning we shower, drink coffee and go to Stinson Beach. It's crowded, sticky and beautiful, with the mountain kissing the sand behind us. Straight ahead is Hawaii, and further on, Japan, with its mushroom clouds. Now, that's a place for deformities, not imitations like me. Perhaps if I could get cancer from drinking Strontium 90 milk, I might gain an official place in the roster of world suffering.

Ron lies beside me, eyes closed to the sun, tapping out a tune on his chest. We're both wearing his undershirts and cut-off jeans. He doesn't talk very much, which is fine. I feel occasional waves of nausea from being near him, but he doesn't seem to notice.

There are a lot of couples with children on the beach. It makes me sad watching them. It's a world I've never known. They play in mixed groups: big and small people, adults as well as children dragging buckets of water to make elaborate castles with moats and tunnels. Parents and children together chase balls, laugh, push each other or hold earnest conversations, listening intently to what the other has to say. Fathers are as involved as mothers, everyone glistening in

87

their California tans. I feel white and worm-like, from a much colder planet.

"You're getting burned," says Ron and closes his eyes again.

At least he has noticed something. I walk to the water. It's warmer than I thought it would be, than the lake was.

"You're pretty red," says a short-haired woman playing with a baby near my feet.

"Thanks."

I turn and get Ron to take me back to San Francisco.

"Thanks for carting me around. I won't ask you up, though. I really want a nap. That is, unless of course you want to see Taye. She might be home."

He's embarrassed by my awkwardness.

"Listen, Snow, when I want to see Taye I'll arrange to see Taye. I enjoyed being with you and I hope you did with me. I know sometimes I'm not very good company, don't talk, disappear into myself. Taye helped me discover that I do that."

He laughs and looks at his hands, still on the wheel.

"I think you're very nice, Snow."

"No, I'm not."

He doesn't hear what I say.

"Taye was pregnant and I couldn't decide whether I wanted her to have the baby or not, so she had an abortion. Then it was over between us."

"You don't need to be telling me this."

"I think I do."

He glances over and catching his eyes, I can almost like him. Maybe if I pretend that I never slept with him it will be all right.

"Bye, Ron. Stay in touch."

"Did he tell you about the almost baby?" asks Taye that evening.

"Yes. I didn't want him to."

"I wish I'd been strong enough to have it without him, but I wasn't. My group promised to give me emotional support and all that, but I just couldn't trust they'd be around for the next eighteen years until whatever it was grew up. When I was married my husband didn't want a child either. It's a real test for them. They can't bullshit so easily when it comes to a child. All of a sudden they have to start taking it more seriously, not just stick it in and forget it. They have to decide how much they're going to commit. Most of them, either physically or emotionally, take a permanent dive. I'll tell you, for me a relationship either has to go forward or stagnate. And I'm just about convinced that men get to a certain place and they're simply not biologically equipped to go on from there. Women are an evolutionary step ahead and there's nothing much to do about it. Maybe in a couple of generations they'll catch up."

She takes a long drag of her joint.

"I doubt it, though."

"I feel funny that I was with him, that you take it so easily. You put him down but you hug him and you also wanted to have his baby. Aren't you jealous?"

"Why? He doesn't want to have a baby with you, does he? If that was happening I guess I'd be upset. Now I just feel sorry for him. For you too, if you want anything more from him, because you won't get it, the same way I don't. I guess, in a way, I like to see him going through other women and nothing happening. I get reassured that it's not me who's nuts, but him."

She takes another drag.

"Wow, that's awful what I just said. Forget what I said. Don't tell my group I said that. That was a very unliberated thing to say. Oh dear, I probably have to tell them that I said it."

She passes me the joint and we listen to Joan Baez, "All my troubles soon be over."

I look up and catch Taye staring at me.

"Snow, the time has come for you to meet the group. We're having our annual women's camping trip in a couple of weeks. It'll be the group and friends, by invitation only. Consider yourself invited."

I find the dirty magazine in my dresser drawer. I wish I could have a black bar over my eyes like they do. I feel so tender inside, alone and unprotected. Tonight, when the Nazis come, they'll see the wickedness in my eyes and rip open my stomach as punishment. Will Langley know?

"Okay, trainees," says Langley, "incubation period is over. When you walk out the door today, you'll be trading in your pink beanie forever. Tomorrow morning, when you come in after your first day solo in the field, you'll be wearing green, signifying your arrival on the Ladder of Advancement. I wish all of you success and fulfillment.

"Again I want to acknowledge this morning's achievement story. It was a fine example of productive goal-setting. You should all remember it, today as you search for your Connect, and tonight in your individual search for positive creative experience."

We sing:

> This is my oath
> I come from GROWTH
> To win the game
> Just sign your name.
> To free the ropes

We must have hopes.

Ya, ya, ya.

I catch Franny on the way out.

"Wait for me this afternoon. I want to talk to you."

"Snow, I'm scared of dogs."

"Think poisoned dog food. They won't touch you. Good luck, kid!"

Langley materializes from nowhere.

"You can't wish good luck for another person. You know that. We all make our own Destiny. I want both you and Franny to remember that today."

I look away from his eyes, trying to hide my torn membrane.

"Can we say 'Break a leg'? Is that okay, Mr. Langley, sir?" asks Franny.

He laughs. "Now you be a good girl, Franny, and we'll have those extra pounds off you in no time."

He walks away.

"Who was that masked man? They really must have our beanies bugged. Take care, Snow. I'll wait for you after."

Bridget drives to an abandoned field near our group's target suburban tract. We gather in a tight huddle, arms around shoulders, and in a whisper the four others chant to me:

It's your day, Snow
Hip hip hurray, Snow
Sock it to 'em
Talk it to 'em
Nice girls finish first.

It's your day, Snow
Better than a lay, Snow
Bright smile, head high

Green grass, blue sky
Nice gals finish first.

"Thanks."

I feel teary-eyed. They drop me at my starting corner. I have five hours on my own before meeting them at the pickup place. They drive off, thumbs raised in salute. Taking a deep breath, I assault my first house.

"Hi, I've been asked to call on mothers in the area. May I step in?"

Without a word, she closes the door in my face.

The eleventh house is a Bingo. It's my Connect, exactly as Langley described her this morning. She's overweight but not obese, wearing a flowered muumuu to the floor. About twenty-five years old, she has laugh lines around her eyes, which are her best feature: large, brown and welcoming. Her light-brown hair is in a ponytail. Holding a coffee mug in one hand, she opens the screen door with the other. On her feet are large, pink, shaggy house slippers.

"Hi," she says.

"Hi, I've been asked to call on mothers in the area. May I step in?"

I walk in as I say it, feeling totally comfortable. Langley has conjured this woman and put her out here to wait for me. Our business is already concluded. Now we merely go through the formalities.

She ushers me into her living room and brings me a cup of coffee. The room is clean, almost sterile, its most significant feature a baby in diaper and undershirt entrapped in a wooden playpen. There are no paintings or posters on the walls. On the shelves there are a few knickknacks, but no books. Starched curtains flutter in the breeze. She sets my cup down on a coaster, so as not to damage the gleaming polish of her coffee table.

"As I said, I'm calling on mothers in this area. Before I go any further, I'll ask a few questions to make sure you qualify for our new pre-school education program."

She nods her acceptance and answers. Her name is Nancy Petrie. She has one child and is pregnant with another. Her husband works in a factory and earns in the $6,000-$8,000 income bracket. They have debts. She gives positive responses to the questions on her interest in education, answering almost word perfect, according to the script. Even the baby is totally cooperative, gurgling in his playpen.

I move to the next stage.

"I represent an organization called GROWTH. You've perhaps heard of Operation Headstart? Well, our materials are similar, except that they are uniquely designed for each mother to use with her child in the privacy of her home."

I reach into my attaché case and remove Demo Chart #1, open it and lay it expertly on the table.

"On this chart you can see a graphic representation of your child's basic developmental growth stages, from the sensory motor up to abstract thinking."

I move my finger from top to bottom as I speak, thus focusing Nancy's attention on the relaxing greens and blues of the chart. I pause long enough for her to read the bold-face type and be lulled by the sea colors, as I time my breathing pattern to hers and then point to a line exactly two-thirds of the way down.

"The focus of GROWTH's program is here, at the interface between pre-cognitive and cognitive, when your child is beginning to think."

As I speak I remove Demo Chart #2 and spread its soft browns and golds on the coffee table.

"We are talking about a child anywhere between one and a half and four years old. In this important transition period, the human brain is more open to absorbing knowledge than it will ever be again."

Nancy glances at her baby, absorbed in chewing a rubber bunny.

"Now, Nancy," I move to the still warmer yellows and oranges of Demo #3, "from your answers I've ascertained that you and your child do qualify for participation in GROWTH's pre-school program."

We share a smile.

"With your permission, I will now introduce you to the format."

Again I match breathing, then slow mine, and Nancy automatically follows, and slows hers.

"As you see, the program is divided into three processes. First, beginning here on the left, is information gathering. Process one is implemented by a developmentally-graded set of children's encyclopedias."

I pause to let her skim the titles of the books.

"Process two is the expansion of creative awareness and ability, implemented by exposure to selections from the world's best children's literature, contained in a ten-volume set."

This time I pause and count one potato, two potato, up to thirty in my head.

"And now process three: instruction and mastery, or control. The material for this process will be sent to you on an on-going basis over the entire three-year period of the program. You will order state-of-the-art records, tapes, films and booklets for your child. Concrete exercises and activities will help him incorporate the learned material into his repertoire."

I give her enough time to gaze at the small print and see that there are dozens of topics listed.

"So, Nancy, how are you impressed by the GROWTH program?"

"Oh, very."

"Well then, let's just finish up the registration details, and you and your family can consider yourselves enrolled."

I pull out the contract form and set it to one side on the table.

"There is one more thing that perhaps needs explanation, and that is your participation dues. Here's a little gimmick we've worked out so that you hardly notice the expense."

I hand her a yellow and orange can with a happy face on it.

"Every day, except for Sundays, you put a dollar in this can. At the end of the month, you send GROWTH a money order for twenty-five dollars. That's it."

I pick up the contract form.

"So if you would help me fill out the registration details."

Her responses continue to flow and as we reach the home stretch, I focus my attention on the dotted line at the bottom of the page.

"And now, Nancy, we need your signature here."

With my right hand I hold out the pen to her and with my left index finger I point to the space. I don't look at her, but focus my total concentration on that dotted line and project her signature onto it. Her fingers brush mine as she takes the pen and then she's writing her name on the page. I feel like laughing and jumping in the air. I've done my part, and I've done it perfectly.

I leave Nancy with her yellow and orange can and Demo Chart, trying not to chatter in my excitement. The sun is shining outside as I walk towards the next house. But I can't figure out how to open the gate and then, suddenly, I feel like I can't move.

Forcing my way to the curb, I sit down and realize I have tears in my eyes. The elation of the sale is totally gone. I sit there and wait for my pickup, reviewing from a grandstand men in black shirts waving red banners with swastikas.

"Have a hard day, Snow?" asks Bridget. "Don't let it get to you. It takes a while to get into the swing of things."

"Bridget's the only one in the car who managed a sale today," says another.

"No, it's not that," I mumble. "I did sell one."

"You did what?!" they scream.

"I finished a sale."

"Well, what are you doing with that look of death-warmed-over, child?"

Bridget can barely keep her hands on the wheel.

"Why didn't you say so before? You're a very strange one. A sale on her first day out, an honor to her entire car group, and she forgets to mention it."

I push myself up against the car door as far as I can, feeling more nauseous by the minute.

"Bridget, she doesn't look well," says the girl next to me.

"I don't feel well. I haven't felt well ever since I left that house. As if I did something bad. I gotta get home and sleep."

"Oh oh." Bridget's voice is motherly. "This sounds like a case for Langley. We'll get you in to him as soon as we get back."

CHAPTER 11

"So, Snow," says Langley, "you made your first sale today and you feel miserable."

I smile, embarrassed for many reasons. He rises from his well-ordered desk-top and leather swivel-chair and comes to sit next to me on the matching leather sofa. A metal standing lamp, a coffee table with an outsized, immaculately clean ashtray and three thriving plants complete the decor. I think of Franny's look, both jealous and congratulatory, as I entered the office with Langley.

"Snow, you can look at me. I'm not going to bite you. I'm very proud of you. In fact, tomorrow you'll be skipping the green beanie altogether and going straight to red, joining the ranks of those who've broken the ice."

"Thank you."

I manage to look at him for a split second. He's looking warm and friendly.

"I guess you think I'm pretty crazy."

"Well, maybe a little," he chuckles and I feel worse. "I'll tell you exactly what I think is happening to you. And please believe me, I really do understand it."

I feel like a drowning person who sees a rescue ship on

the horizon. He walks over to his desk, opens a drawer and takes out a file folder. Sitting a little closer to me on the sofa, he removes a page.

"Take a look at this."

He holds the page so I can read it too, his head not far from mine. I can smell the after shave mixed with Langley's smell and feel the warmth of his body energy mixing with mine. It's very hard to concentrate on reading.

A list of words runs down the page:

SELF-ACTUALIZATION
POTENCY
ACTION
CONTROL
AWARENESS
INSIGHT
DISTURBANCE
ANXIETY
DESPAIR
APATHY

"You are here," says Langley and points to DISTURBANCE.

"And moving on down."

"Not necessarily. Nothing's static. You can go either way."

He sits back, leaving the list and me at the coffee table, giving me room to regain some balance after the closeness of him.

"From what both you and Bridget have described to me, I can analyze your feelings in the following way. By making the sale today, you chose to break out of whatever old patterns you were running, pick yourself up out of free-floating anxiety and move into something new. Quite understandably, you feel shaken and upset, having broken your failure neural patterns, by succeeding. You're following me?"

I nod. Everything he says makes sense. And of more importance is the fact that his entire attention is fixed on me. I've never felt attention like this: a total being with me and not sending parts of his head off in other directions. I feel like a small flower being watered. He continues talking.

"In this last period of time, your mind has been constantly bombarded with new information. You are being challenged and forced to look at yourself in a new way. In doing so, you are discovering sources of strength you had no idea you had, putting them to the test and seeing undeniable, concrete results."

Langley pauses until I look and let him hold my eyes. He demands I see the solidity and sparkle there, and he orders me to bathe in them.

"In this phase of DISTURBANCE you have not yet integrated the new information. The old rules no longer apply, but you have not yet reached the personal INSIGHT that will allow you to assimilate your new knowledge and create new, more appropriate structures. DISTURBANCE is a time of breakdown of the defenses that up until now have worked to preserve the status quo. Without these defenses, a person always feels vulnerable and extra sensitive. Sometimes this is accompanied by strange visions and occurrences that are difficult to explain rationally."

"I see Nazis marching."

Langley smiles, knowingly.

"I do feel better having talked to you, though a little guilty at having taken up your time."

"Just a very little guilt, I hope. It's been my pleasure."

I'm looking down at the floor, so it's a total surprise when I feel his fingers brush my cheek, and a shock of electricity runs down my spine.

"You are very special, Snow. You know, of all the GROWTH people, at this moment, I feel the closest to you."

I look into his eyes.

"I'd like to kiss you," he says.

I let his hand pull me forward and we kiss; softly, briefly, and he lets me go. I feel flushed and frightened.

"Oh dear."

"Don't be afraid, Snow. What is between us just is. Nothing to do or not do. I guess we'd better go now. Are you okay?"

"Fine. Sure. I'm already on my way. Uh, see you tomorrow at the meeting. Thanks."

I run all the way home, not aware of anything until I'm in my room, curled on my bed in fetal position and able to observe the flashes of heat and lightning that crash through me.

When I manage to ground the electricity, I call Franny in Berkeley.

"I'm in the middle of making granola," she answers. "But who cares! What happened with you? What happened with Langley? I heard you made a sale today. Is that why you went in there? Is he real or is there some switch in his office that turns him on and off?"

"Slowly. It wasn't that big a deal. He just calmed me down some. I'm calling because I want to come across the bay and visit you."

"Sure. That'd be great. But if you stay overnight, I've got to check with the others."

"What others?"

"I told you. I live in a commune thing, a collective. We have to check about overnight guests."

"But you're not a real hippie, are you?"

"No, I'm just fat. Ha, ha. I wash and everything. But I will warn you about one thing, you have to eat only health food while you're in the house. Or else we can go out to Oscar's for hamburgers. When you coming?"

"It depends. See, I need your help with something while I'm there."

There's a pause, and then her voice cracks as she makes it into a joke.

"Oh, Snow, and I thought it was purely a friendly visit."

She sounds like I've killed her dog.

"Franny, it is friendly. I feel very close to you. It's just I don't know many people here and I need help with something."

I realize I'm making it worse.

"Forget what I said. Let's start over . . . "

She stops me.

"Hey, I'm a diagnosed paranoid. Don't feed the fire by acting like you've really done something wrong. You're supposed to tell me I'm nuts, not feel guilty about it. Now say it nice and clear, 'Franny, you're nuts.' "

"Franny, you're nuts."

"There, don't I feel better now? What can I do for you?"

"Birth control. My Canadian prescription ran out and I need some new pills."

Why do I lie? Will I ever learn not to be embarrassed by innocence?

"Hey, no sweat. I can even take you to the clinic and you won't have to pay a cent. Come over after work tomorrow and we'll go to the evening check-up. Are you sure this isn't connected to Langley?"

"I only wish it was. But it isn't. And I don't want a check-up."

"You have to. They won't give you pills if you don't. It's mainly to check for crabs and a Wasserman to see if you've got V.D."

"Oh God." I wish I had the nerve to ask what a Wasserman is.

"Hey, Snow, I see you're already finding your way about the city. Somebody special?"

"Just want to be prepared, you know. Are you on the pill?"

"No, I've got a loop. My matings are so few and far between it'd be a shame to have to remember to take pills all the time for them."

I don't ask what a loop is either. I do tell her about the sale and feeling bad and Langley working with me to understand why. I don't mention his touch.

"I want some time alone with Langley too. I think I'll answer his invitation and make an appointment to further discuss the plans for my excess poundage."

I flash a picture of Franny sitting on the leather couch with Langley.

"He is married, isn't he?" I ask.

"Sure. You think a hunk like that is going to be walking around free? My car boss told me. It was the first question I asked. Two girl progeny too. I wonder what his wife thinks about the whole GROWTH set-up. All that nubile flesh."

"She's probably the mousy, devote-her-whole-life-to-the-King type. Perfect faith and all that. Do you think he plays around?"

"Oh, he must. Just pray to God that we'll be among the Chosen."

Why do I lie to Franny? It isn't fair hiding information when she thinks I'm being open with her. But she has her covers too. I can feel them. So why shouldn't I have mine? What Langley does with me is my own business. And, furthermore, I am making a very big deal out of a touch on the cheek. A pat on the back is what it was, job well done. There is no reason Langley Keel would start with me when he's got a city of sophisticated women to choose from.

"Are you home?" calls Taye.

"Yeah. I'm just taking a casserole out of the oven for us. Do you like tuna?"

"From what you've told me about your job, which is very little," says Taye sucking a noodle, "it seems that you and I are both upset by the feeling of exploitation. I myself am finding it harder and harder to give out those contest vouchers. I smile and say, 'Do business with us. It's worth your while,' and inside I'm very conflicted."

"It's a living, like any other. If you're good at it, you make money. It seems fairly straightforward to me now."

"Snow, you're turning out to be a lot stronger than I thought. You want a yogurt for dessert?"

"Pineapple."

"I personally am thinking of quitting my job. There are a couple of other women who are opening a women's book-store: espresso machine, luxurious spaces to sit, poetry reading in the evening with people like Judy Chicago. You don't know who she is, do you?"

This time I opt for honesty.

"You're right I don't know who she is. But, Taye, I want to tell you something. Sometimes you make me feel like a real idiot – like I got caught not doing my homework. It's really not my fault that I didn't grow up in the heartland of West Coast culture."

She laughs.

"Step one is knowing that you don't know."

She spoons up some yogurt.

"Snow, you know that as a sister I feel this responsibility to educate and at the same time I try not to get too involved. So sometimes it comes out harsh. I have to watch myself. I have a tendency to over-commit and that's bad for my health. It's not so good for yours either, by the way. And yet sometimes you show these terrible trenches of ignorance

103

that scream to be filled and, Jesus Christ, you pretend they're not even there. I'm going to be frank with you, Snow. I feel you're putting on a show. Inside you believe you're better than anybody else, but you go around looking all meek and child-like. Then, when you find the soft spot, you bite. I only say this to you because I've discovered you're strong enough to hear it."

I choke on a piece of pineapple. I don't know what to do. If I cry I'll be proving her weakness point, so I make noises about tiredness and thank her for the interesting analysis.

I don't quite know what happened to invite the attack. I shouldn't have been honest about Judy Chicago. I shouldn't have slept with Ron. Taye sounded like a mother I once overheard while she was pushing a kid in a shopping cart in Loblaws. In the same cold, matter-of-fact voice as Taye, the mother said to her five-year-old: "You're not to be trusted. You're a liar. Nobody should believe you. Your father believes you, but he's wrong."

I should be angry at Taye for what she said, like I was angry at the mother in the supermarket. But I'm not.

There's too much truth in it to feel angry. My own mother would agree with her completely. The only mistake Taye made is saying that I think I'm better than others. But no matter, the poison comes out the same. So Taye's learned I am mean and garbage-like. This is no news to me. I am but a vessel, ejecting evil on automatic pilot.

Undressed in bed, I let my hand wander my face to the cheek that Langley stroked, and then to my lips. By the rules of my mind, I'm not allowed to imagine anything further. If I do, it's a guarantee that what's seen in my head will never happen in the real world. But I want to be bad, so I change Langley to my math teacher and let his hand stray to my breast. The nipple grows hard as he strokes it and both breasts start to swell until they're like ripe melons bursting out of the top of my dress, like in the *Playboy* cartoons. I roll onto my stomach as I let my hand move lower, swaying on my giant breasts and pushing my pillow under my stomach to create balance. I am bad, sucked and fondled, and it feels so good. All those who hate me watch disgusted at my pleasure, and anger brings me to a warm and sticky finish, a grin going lengthwise down my body.

Oh dear, I've rated the death penalty again. I guess I can always get a job bombing Cambodians.

CHAPTER 12

I receive two notes. One is left on the kitchen table.

Snow–
I want to apologize for laying into you last night.
I meant to be offering comfort and support, and
instead it came out attacking you. I plan to work
on this in group. Please try and forget what I
said, or at least accept it as the words of a mad-
woman who has now returned to her more-sane
self and would like to be your friend.
Taye

The other is given to me by Laurie after I hand back my red beanie.

Snow, thank you for sharing with me.
Langley

I'm high all day and without effort make another sale. Franny is worshipful as we take the bus to Berkeley, looking at me with shining eyes.

"Listen, Snow, you've got to give me some tips on how you do it."

"I'll be honest with you, Franny. I don't understand what's happening myself. Since I've come to San Francisco, my luck's changed or something. People respond to me like I was really somebody, believe in me. Or maybe it's just they see how naive I am and try to help me out."

She looks at me critically.

"You may be right. There is something in you, Snow, that calls forth the nurturing and instructing impulse. I feel it even as we speak and am motivated to fill you in on the inside dope about the East Bay. Are you ready? As we drive into Berkeley, we will cross the Bay Bridge on the *lower* level. It's not like it was filmed in *The Graduate*, with Dustin Hoffman racing after Mrs. Robinson's daughter into Berkeley, across the top level. Top level is for traffic going in the direction of San Francisco."

The lower level of the bridge turns out to be entirely enclosed: a tunnel. It sucks us in and then expels us into the end of daylight at the other side. My first glimpse of the East Bay is a disappointment. Instead of the Mecca of student consciousness, I get more middle-class suburbia.

Franny sees me looking forlornly out the window.

"Hey, cheer up. We've not yet arrived at the center of the cosmos. We're coming in at the bus station, in the flatlands. This is a low-rent area that is devoid of all spiritual enlightenment, pre Baba Ram Dass, if you know what I mean. We have to change buses to reach Berkeley itself. Then we'll go straight to Northside, where I live. South of the campus is déclassé – hard drugs and maniacs."

The Berkeley bus pulls first into Shattuck Avenue, which still looks like a shopping street anywhere. But then we make a right turn and as we climb the hill, my expectations begin to be fulfilled: strangely painted redwood houses, shops with hand-lettered signs and people in hippie clothes, like on television. We get off at the supermarket.

"The natives are quiet," says Franny. "No posters up for rioting in the streets today. Besides, it's summer session at school, so most of the radical left is off camping or visiting their parents."

She guides me through the parking lot to the store.

"This is the Co-op. We own shares here. I have to pick up some vegetables and we'll buy some Pepperidge Farm cookies to gorge ourselves on in secret after the stuffed zucchini dinner."

In front of the grocery store are dogs, all kinds of dogs. There are dogs tied to trees and poles and front fenders. There are wandering dogs sniffing, licking and chasing each other. There are dogs fondling the occasional human. And there are boxes and boxes of puppy dogs to be given away. One especially enormous dog is chasing a frisbee thrown by an especially enormous man in a Bedouin robe.

We enter the store and I'm comforted by the familiar act of taking a shopping cart. This feeling of familiarity lasts for about ten seconds.

"We really look abnormal."

At first Franny looks puzzled, then catches on.

"Oh, you mean our clothes."

We're both wearing Peter Pan collar, tailored blouses. I've got on a pastel, pleated skirt. Franny's in too-tight blue cotton pants with a side zipper. Every other human being in the Co-op, shopper and worker, is either wearing blue jeans and a T-shirt or a floor-length robe.

"Don't worry, Snow. A lot of folks wear a straight uniform to work. Just pretend you're a nurse."

I make the push bar of the cart the focal point for reality, and attempt to incorporate what lies around me into structures known to my brain. The people are connected with life as I regularly know it. Like in Loblaws, they are shopping for groceries, wiping kids' noses, checking out shopping bags, deciding on which flavor of Campbell's soup and wheeling their carts through the aisles, avoiding collisions. So what's making my mind not compute? Finally it clicks. In this supermarket nobody's over thirty years old. There aren't any grownups.

"Everybody takes turns helping, cutting up cheese or bringing in the produce from the farms or something," says Franny.

We take our groceries and walk through lamplit, tree-lined streets. It's warm, and people are outside strumming guitars, talking, eating and smoking. The sweet smell of marijuana fills the air. Initially there's an appearance of openness and accessibility. But I quickly realize the defined sense of privacy that exists beneath it. There is a deep respect for separate space systems. Groups acknowledge our passing; but each cluster is a solar system, and each person within the cluster is his own solar center. There is a finely tuned awareness to others orbiting nearby, with an implicit understanding of non-aggression.

"It's really a special place, isn't it?" smiles Franny. "Here's my house."

Blood-curdling screams pour out of the two-storied white house.

"That's Sid. He's in Primal Scream Therapy. Don't let it bother you."

I try to act nonchalant as we cross the side veranda and enter the unlocked house. The screams are coming from the basement and I'm happy that after she sets the groceries in the kitchen Franny leads me up the staircase to her room, a large space under the roof with a window set in the slanted ceiling.

"Listen, dinner's in about half an hour. Then we'll walk over to the clinic. I'm going to change and see if they need any help in the kitchen."

"You've got a great room."

I move closer to a dark-wood coffee table with a lighter inlay of a hand-painted scene of courtly lovers.

"I got that at the Alameda flea market. Why don't you prowl around a little and come on down when you're ready. I'll give you a pair of jeans to change into: dream jeans that I plan to wear one day when I'm thin."

Franny changes clothes, and so as not to embarrass her, I turn and study her bookshelves, full of positive-thinking and diet manuals. There is no mirror here.

"See you in the kitchen."

She leaves in loose jeans and a man's workshirt, looking twice the size she did when we came in. On a brass bed covered by a patchwork quilt, she's left me a pair of neatly folded blue jeans. They are too big, but manageable.

I check out the last item of furniture in the room, a small roll-top desk, on top of which are three framed pictures. Each one is of the same strained smiling older couple and a different child. Franny is the oldest of the children, and the heaviest.

The screams have softened into whimpers, so I gather courage and venture downstairs.

The kitchen is the cooking, eating and meeting place; bright and noisy. The cooking is overseen by a tall, yellow-bearded, Jesus-looking guy, who, bare to the waist, stirs a large pot with one hand and waves at a tiny, pretty woman cutting up vegetables with the other.

"Big chunks. I insist on big chunks."

I move towards Franny, who is working at a round oak table, beautifully refinished and surrounded by carved wooden chairs. She is transferring whole black peppers from a glass jar to a pepper mill.

"Can I do something?"

"Introduce yourself to tonight's cooking team, George and Colette, and set the table. We're nine all together."

George points me to a cupboard where I find an assortment of handmade, clay plates and to a drawer with flatware. He opens the oven door, and the smell of the stuffed zucchini conjures up five more people: introduced as Sid the screamer, Jeannie the poet, Bruce the lawyer, Cathy the clown, and Peewee the rabbi. We sit, and George and Colette serve vegetable soup, salad and zucchini, accompanied by thick slices of homemade whole wheat bread.

"George, you've once again surpassed yourself," says Franny. "How am I supposed to lose weight around here?"

"Eat less," says Sid.

"Don't buy garbage cookies," says George.

"See what a supportive environment I live in, Snow?"

The rest of the meal is eaten in almost silence, but not an uncomfortable one. I help clear and wash and dry. Inside the Berkeley house I feel the same atmosphere as I did outside. The eight move instinctively around each other; without touching, neither imposing nor inviting. Franny's sometimes boisterousness is the exception, and she herself grows more subdued as the East Bay vibes soak into her.

We walk to the clinic, also a redwood house, set back on a well-kept lawn. Franny's unfamiliar silence makes me nervous. I wish she would give me more helpful information for my first gynecological visit.

Inside, the waiting room is cheerful enough: freshly painted, nice chairs and posters on the walls. One is especially eye-catching: of a tough-looking Negro man with a swelling belly and the caption, "WOULD YOU BE MORE CARE-FUL IF THIS HAPPENED TO YOU?"

A nurse ushers me through swinging doors and into one of the cubicles that line the inner corridor. A padded table with two gleaming metal stirrups confronts me. She opens a large piece of tissue paper with a hole in the middle.

"Take off your clothes and put this over your head."

She leaves and I follow instructions. Not wanting to get near that table, I wait, leaning on the wall. Eventually the door opens.

"Why are you just standing there? Is this your first visit?"

The doctor is young, probably an intern. He smiles when I nod yes to his question, and motions me to get up on the table. I sit on the edge, not knowing what to do.

"Slide all the way down to the bottom and put your legs into the stirrups. I know it's not very dignified, but it's effi-cient."

I can't believe this is standard procedure. Do they do this to my mother?

I lie staring up at the overhead fluorescents, wishing that I was a man. The doctor sits between my legs and puts on a surgical glove. I whimper.

"Don't be frightened, dear. I'm going to gently check in there, make sure everything's okay. If you'd like, I can fix up a mirror so you can watch."

"God, no!"

He laughs and pushes the fingers of his hand inside me, the other hand on my pelvis.

"Now try and relax. Breathe deeply. That's a good girl. See, you can even learn to enjoy it."

He presses on my belly.

"Now, I'm going to clamp you open."

Something cold grips me.

"And insert a piece of cotton with this forceps to take a

112

Pap smear to make sure everything's okay. There we go. All done. You're not very experienced, are you?"

"Not very."

"I don't know how much you know about this clinic, but we consider ourselves to be not only a medical but an educational institution. Our purpose is to help make sex a creative and joyful experience. We dispense birth control devices to prevent unwanted pregnancies and we also instruct women about their bodies."

"That's nice."

I'm having rather a hard time talking normally to a man who's sitting between my legs.

"What I'll do now, during the second part of your checkup, is verify that you're aware of your clitoris. If you're like many of our first-timers, you've probably never masturbated all the way to orgasm."

I'm too shocked to correct him. He touches me gently.

"Every woman must learn her own rhythms, but most of you are so anxious to please that you never take the time to do this."

He's stroking me as he talks.

"Now close your eyes. We have all the time in the world. You can relax. I'm not going to have intercourse with you. You're not going to pay me back. This is a lesson that I'm happy to provide, an essential part of your examination. Don't do anything, but feel my fingers touching you. If you'd like it faster or slower, then tell me."

Is this guy a pervert, or is this standard Berkeley service? I'll probably never have the courage to find out. I raise my head to see his face. He looks stern and professional, concentrating on his work. I lie back and observe his technique.

"A little slower," I tell him.

The only sound is the ticking of the clock. I can't fake anything; he'll be able to tell. He's so earnest, I don't want to hurt his feelings. If only I had my pillow! At last, I finally feel the tissue swelling, and then the gradual release.

He pats my head and hands me a plastic-wrapped sponge.

"That was what's called an orgasm. It is a healthy, normal experience. Come back in three months for another check-up."

Rinsed and dressed, I exit shakily and the nurse takes me to another cubicle for a blood test, which she explains is for V.D.

The last cubicle contains the social worker.

"Pills," I answer.

"You get three months' worth."

She hands me three green plastic wheels, with little yellow pills in them. The first two letters of a day of the week are stamped above each pill.

"Always begin seven days after your period starts, and always take your pill at the same time of day, so you won't forget. The first month we recommend use of a diaphragm along with the pill. In three months, you can come for an examination and a renewal of your prescription. That's it. You can go now."

I make my way out to Franny.

"Everything okay? You were in there a long time."

"The doctor was into education. Gave me everything but the slide show."

"There's a lot of turnover there. Each guy with his own shtick."

My body still tingling with after-shock, I let it go at that.

Franny and I drink tea and nibble cookies, and then share her brass bed. I haven't slept with a girlfriend since I was twelve.

"I'm sorry I take up so much room," she says.

"Franny, you're obsessed. Before I visited you I had no

idea of the interesting life you lead. All you talked about was fat and diets. And now I see you all involved in the Berkeley stuff. I'm really jealous."

"What's to be jealous of? Knowing a bunch of crazy people? I'll tell you, Snow, I have much more reason to be jealous. You're starting a thing with Langley, aren't you?"

It's dark and we can't see each other, and it's like being twelve again, when it was safe to talk.

"I don't think so. He was nice to me and made me feel better. I was having some kind of weird reaction after my first sale and I got all upset. I think it's all part of his job."

"No, it's not just that. You know it too."

"Listen, I'm not going to let myself in for total humiliation, thinking that anything special is happening when it isn't. He's got an army of women panting for him. There's no way he'd invest time with me."

"Wouldn't it be lovely, though?"

"Yes, Franny. Goodnight."

I try to push him out. But my body overrules and allows Langley in, his kiss and the intern's fingers intertwine. I call on my math teacher, but this time he fails me and refuses to come. I'm falling and my fail-safe mechanisms are on the blink.

CHAPTER 13

*L*ife is a mysterious thing. You spend your whole time trying to get some control over a little bit of it, get it organized so you can make a plan or two, and then *wham*, it hits you with an event you weren't ready for. I'm not exactly complaining because most of the time I'm hungry for the unexplained and unexpected. But you can bet as soon as the unpredictable happens, I'll feel crazy until I can get it into some kind of framework again.

Langley hands me a note asking me out to dinner; to wait downstairs at the restaurant after work. I sit outside, sip a cold lemonade and try to make order out of chaos. He has violated the boss-being-thoughtful-to-his-employee system. I have to invent a new cosmology. However, I'm caught in a philosophical bind. If I invent a new system, I commit hubris, and invite destruction. I am allowed to create sense only in retrospect. So meanwhile I have to live the present and stay feeling crazy.

To block my head from future pictures, I concentrate on what is around me: my drink and its tiny pieces of floating lemon, the ice cubes with holes in the middle that you can stick the straw through and pick up, the white metal table covered by a red-and-white checkered tablecloth, a napkin holder, an ashtray and glass salt and pepper shakers. The hard, white chair hurts the back of my legs. I feel swollen before my period; a pimple is starting over my left eyebrow.

There are voices around me: a conversation between two men about selling a plot of land in Mendocino, a couple who don't say much, except every few minutes he breaks the silence by whispering, "Are you sure?" and she murmurs back, "Yes, I think so."

I remember the sale I made today to an older woman with seven children, and I fill up my head with the details so successfully that I don't even feel Langley come to my table.

"May I sit down? I'm very glad you agreed to meet me. Would you like another drink?"

I realize I'm sipping at an empty glass.

"I'm taking you to a place in Sausalito to eat, but we can have a drink here."

He orders two glasses of red wine and I finally meet his eyes. We look for a few seconds, and then he reaches out and again, in one slow downward motion, strokes my cheek. He withdraws his hand, but the warmth stays.

"I don't mean to scare you. I've been thinking about doing that all day." He smiles shyly. "Listen, Snow, I know what you're thinking. You're wondering why I picked you to get close to, right? But at the same time you also know why."

There is silence. Some kind of response seems called for, so I gather my strength and clear my throat to get the quaver out of it.

"You're right about the not knowing, and wrong about the also knowing. I don't know why you asked me to meet you. I probably sound naive, but that's the truth. I don't know why we're sitting here, and I don't know why you kissed me yesterday and why you touched my cheek just now. Unless it's that you're trying out some kind of new training tech-

117

nique on me. It seems to be working because I keep making sales. I hope that's not true."

The drinks come. Langley sips his wine for a while and cloaks me in a fond, fatherly gaze.

After a long time he says, "No. I'm not working on a training technique. This is just personal: Langley wanting to know Snow because she interests him. As a woman interests a man. Now let's go."

He guides me, with his hand pressing gently in the small of my back, to an underground parking garage and a white Peugeot. In a series of fluid motions, he tosses my attaché case in the back of the car, guides me into the front, settles himself on the driver's side and turns to me.

"I'd like to kiss you."

At this point I have about as much resistance as a chicken whose head has been put under its wing. It's a long kiss, and despite the handbrake between us, Langley manages to pull me near to him so that our bodies meet and cling. By the time he releases me I'm shaking. He kisses each eyelid softly and puts his hands on the wheel. Then he laughs.

"We'd better get to that restaurant."

We drive in an unambiguous silence. The air between us pulsates, sending little tentacles out to engage and vanquish. We cross the Golden Gate Bridge at sunset and the postcard picture brings whirlpools and wind vectors from other planets. Langley concentrates on the road, just once reaching over and lightly touching my knee.

At the restaurant he opens the door, and again, very softly, lets his hand touch my back to guide me in. Inside, it is bright and noisy. The entrance leads immediately to a long, full bar and a narrow corridor between high wicker stools and stained-glass windows. We navigate the passageway towards the restaurant beyond, passing the overhead television: the sound drowned by the bar noise, a picture of a guy with an American flag on his space suit lumbering about on rocks on the TV screen.

"That's the first man on the moon," says a slurred voice from the bar.

"Really?" says another.

Langley guides me through the tables to a dim and cozy corner behind a giant potted plant. We sit at the small, linen-covered, elegantly set table, a single rose between us.

"I'd forgotten today was Moon Day. Shouldn't we be paying more attention? This is a momentous occasion."

He holds me tight with his eyes and laughs.

"Yes, it is."

I sigh, feeling out of control, inexorably drawn towards the abyss. But I decide to try for a foothold anyway.

"Langley, I want to talk to you a little. Words. Conversation. I don't really care what it's about, as long as it's things that we can both make sentences from. Is that okay?"

He's amused again.

"Of course, Snow. What would you like to talk about?"

"Well, we could talk about the moon. My roommate told me about a friend of hers who's offended by the whole project. Sees it as sexist."

"Why?"

"Because the moon is a female symbol, lunar cycle and all that, and a man shouldn't be up there violating it. I understand what she means. Can you?"

"Sure, I can. But I understand even more why I'm here with you."

"Langley, when you talk like that about you and me, you confuse me."

"I'll try and explain. What you remembered your friend's saying about the moon, the topic for your conversation, it's very special. I felt that specialness in you when you were in my office. The way you listened and felt and took things in.

You were so sweet then, so open, I felt good just being with you. And now too. This doesn't happen to me often these days."

I just laugh.

He suddenly looks like a devastated five-year-old.

"You don't believe me, do you? You think I'm lying?"

I rush to comfort.

"No, it's not that, not really. It's just hard not to see you as getting whatever you want whenever you want it. You want to feel good with a woman, you can have one whenever you like."

His face closes and hardens.

"Maybe we'd better order."

"What did I say wrong? Tell me."

He doesn't answer, letting whatever we had die and wither between us. I can already smell the decay setting in, the carrion birds perched to pick over the sun-bleached bones. I search for courage.

"Langley, this isn't fair. You can at least tell me what I did."

But he stays silent and the waitress arrives.

Pretending to be solicitous of me, he decides on lobster and salad. The wine steward opens and pours a bottle of Chablis. Langley automatically raises his glass and waits for me to raise mine. I do and we drink. He still doesn't speak and his eyes rove between the leaves of our plant, out into the universe beyond.

"All right. I'll guess what's going on. You're a successful, attractive man. But lonely. Everybody thinks you should be happy because you have it all."

His eyes come back behind the plant so I plunge on.

"But you have secret caverns inside that no one knows about. It would scare most people to know they exist, they would abandon you. In me, you see something kindred. From the beginning, I felt you stroke me inside, in a place no one else knows. It's a place I can't tell anybody about. A person knows it or he doesn't. You and I do. And if I say trite things about myself, I deny access to you."

The bronchial tubes between us are open again. Langley's focus is back on me and I can breathe again.

"I'm sorry, Snow. I know I can be a pretty unpleasant person when I feel hurt. But I don't mean to hurt you. I hope you can still like me. At least a little."

"Oh, I do."

I'm pretty scared by now. I've never talked like this to anybody. And I'm still amazed that Langley is showing me secret parts of himself: this hidden, unsure, undefended essence that calls for complete trust in the other. It makes me want to cuddle and hold him.

The lobster and salad are delicious. So are the coffee and chocolate mousse. We don't talk much after passing those hurdles, food punctuated by smiles and giggles.

When it's time to go, Langley pays and steers me back to the car. We sit in the parking lot, looking out the windshield.

"Well, that was very nice," he says. "I'd like to do it again."

"Me too."

He sighs and turns on the ignition.

"I guess this is more complicated than I'm pretending it to be. You know I'm married, don't you?"

"Yes."

"And I'd like to see you some more."

"Yes."

"And it needs to be a secret."

"Yes."

We drive back to San Francisco. I try to sort out my thoughts, make logical constructs, but my focus is disturbed by tingling skin. The cool night air coming in the window plays havoc with my heat-radiating body. Langley concentrates on the driving with an occasional glance over at me.

Once he says, "I can't really believe you're sitting there."

I touch his cheek. I direct him to my house. We pull up in front and I reach for the door handle. He stops me. We sit in silence.

"You want me to ask you in?"

"No. I want to make love with you very much, but not yet. When you and I make love, we'll make the time and environment we deserve. Now I'm just having a hard time leaving you."

We kiss.

"Okay, Snow, you better go in now. Goodnight, darling."

"Goodnight."

And he drives home to his wife and kids. I must be even more of an evil person than I thought I was. His family, for me, is a scheduling problem and that's all. I don't feel guilty. In fact, I feel fantastic. At the moment my only spiritual torment is imagining Langley's lips and fingers in places he doesn't yet know.

I'm proud to be an Other Woman. It's dangerous and romantic. I am both the Sanctuary and the Excitement, providing the elements missing in an otherwise well-ordered life. It is much preferable to being a Wife, the one who keeps the checkbook balanced and the diapers clean.

This beautiful man wants me. Maybe even needs me. Perhaps there is meaning to the Universe, and my wildest fantasies are coming true.

CHAPTER 14

*E*rnie is the only one of my new friends who might understand about Langley and me. I'm not even willing to give Taye or Franny a chance. Taye is too much of an educator. I don't want her cynical attitude about men coloring my own perceptions. And I've figured out why I'm not honest with Franny. She's a voyeur. With her I feel exposed, my privacy pried into without my consent. I'm also disturbed by the thought that perhaps I'm not willing to confide in either of them because they are women. Women are not to be trusted. Any woman will betray another woman for a man. I know these ideas are more than a little sick, but I also know they're there.

I've been eaten from inside with Why can't I be like her? thoughts, wishing my body, my face, my personality were different. I've watched the boys flock around "her," my teachers light up when "she" raised her hand, and I've tried to figure out what it was that I was missing. And sometimes, out of my jealousy, I've wished "her" harm. And from this knowing myself is born my distrust of the other. Now that I'm having my string of luck, my women friends might try and destroy my happiness, to soothe a dark lacking in themselves.

My feelings for Langley must be hidden from Taye and Franny. They would try and talk me out of it for my "own good," their advice perhaps given out of their own needs, and not mine. I was told by many not to ask another girl for suggestions about a hairdo or clothing because she would tell you something that would make you unattractive in order to enhance herself. So of course I shouldn't ask advice about a man.

Do I really believe these things?

For whatever reasons, I now know that only Ernie is safe. He renews his invitation to come with him to the Alameda flea market. Early Sunday morning we cross the Bay Bridge in an old flatbed truck that Ernie's borrowed from a friend.

"You know, in *The Graduate* they filmed this crossing in reverse," he says.

"Yes, I know."

"I brought you fresh figs for breakfast. Have you ever tasted them? And there's a thermos with hot, freshly ground coffee by your feet."

The figs are tart and juicy, the coffee rich. Ernie's also brought a small thermos filled with hot milk, and sugar in a shaker, to make cafe con leche.

"How do you think to do these special things?"

"Long years of neglect, my love, offset by being in the company of cretins and sensual morons. In self-defense I've learned to pay attention to the details of comfort. By the way, I only share with those who notice. That's a compliment, Snow. You can smile."

The day is bright and warm. We pull off the freeway into sleepy suburban streets. Gradually the neighborhood becomes more sparsely populated until we reach open fields and what appears to be a drive-in movie lot. A giant screen overlooks a concrete wall.

"Ernie, this may sound dumb, but this looks like what in Canada we call a drive-in movie."

"Sunday mornings the drive-in is the flea market."

I hear a droning as if from a beehive on the other side of the wall. Ernie takes my hand and walks me through the dust to a small door in the solid concrete.

"Ready? Hold on to your hat!" and he pulls me through.

Spread out before us is an indecipherable mass of things. At first, all I can see are multileveled colors: colors snaking along the ground, colors moving at eye level, colors dancing on platforms in the sky. Slowly I'm able to differentiate between swirling and non-swirling objects. I feel like an ant on a patchwork quilt. If only the space had boundaries, instead of stretching off into limitless horizon with no sign of the rest of the concrete wall.

The drone begins to disentangle into distinct parts. Vague bursts of static evolve into babies' crying, children's calling, animals' scuffling and grownups bargaining. The background continues to hum like the tracks before the subway reaches the station.

My nose is alternately fondled and assaulted by a blend of spice and sweat.

Ernie keeps my hand in his as we stand pressed to the wall, giving me time to get adjusted.

"Ready to walk a little?"

I begin to sense order. The vast area is divided into long dirt corridors, not necessarily parallel, that are bordered by selling spaces. These spaces, one sometimes sliding into the next, are territories defined by the character of the people and goods stationed there. Each unit is portable enough to remove in time for the early movie. A woolen army blanket is spread on the ground to display frayed T-shirts and cut-offs. A coat rack is elegantly laden with 1930's dresses. A frog's mouth, giant and green, stretches out a red tongue on which tiny, carved wooden flies are perched for sale. Every place has its own music: radio, guitar, flute, tape-deck, volumes finely tuned to stay within borders. Some offer food, some coffee, some a comfortable place to sit down.

The proprietors receive customers as if into their homes. Even the guy on the army blanket. The customer, when he enters a space, first makes contact with the owner. He says, "Nice stuff" or "Just looking," and the owner merely nods, but something is exchanged. Only then does he turn to the goods. If he decides to buy, talk starts up again around the price; bargaining to formalize the transaction. Sometimes there are longer conversations, the stories behind the decisions to sell or buy.

Besides the regular folks, there is also a class of professional sellers. Ernie points them out to me. They're scattered through the market, eyes slightly hooded, talking tough or phony sweet, out to make a buck by sucking in the rubes. Most of the crowd steers clear of them.

The flea market is packed with shoppers ranging from flagrant hippies in war paint and beads to suburbanites in imitation madras. There is no shoving or grabbing. People take turns to look, put things back in place when they're finished. I compare it with Honest Ed's bargain basement, where a person is lucky if his eye is not scratched out as he sifts through the merchandise.

"It's wonderful, Ernie. It's so neat being here, I can't even think about buying yet."

"There's a section for food in the middle. Let's go get a sandwich."

I munch egg and bean sprouts on black bread. Ernie chomps down on spicy Italian sausage in a French roll.

"How's your love life?" he asks.

126

Three little kids have encircled me, asking if I want to buy home-baked carob-chip cookies. There is no price. I give them a quarter for two, and they seem satisfied.

"It's clear to me that you're in love."

I laugh.

"As am I," he says in dark seriousness.

"Take me shopping, Ernie. I don't want to think about love right now. You said you'd pick out clothes for me. I brought money and I'm ready to buy."

We move back out into the market, through the furniture section haunted by old dark wooden things with cloudy mirrors, and into the main clothes arena. Racks of clothes, blankets of clothes, chairs of clothes, walls of clothes, ropes of clothes, cars of clothes, trucks of clothes and even one bus of clothes. Ernie doesn't glance at the jeans, India print shirts or Bedouin dresses, but homes right in on a tent with open flaps draped in black velvet.

"Black velvet?"

"A jacket. You'll be able to wear almost any of your regular dowdy wardrobe and with the jacket you'll pass."

He quickly scans the soft display and decides. The nursing owner, sitting cross-legged with her baby in the tent opening, gives him an appreciative look. Ernie fits me into quilted long sleeves puffed at the top and zips the waist-length jacket closed, securing the tiny pearl button at the collar. He steps back to admire his judgment.

"Perfect."

There is no mirror, but I trust him.

"How much?" I ask softly, so as not to disturb the sucking baby.

"Two dollars."

"Dollar and a half," says Ernie before I can take the money out to pay her.

"Dollar seventy-five," she closes the transaction.

"At the flea market you bargain," explains Ernie as we walk away with our purchase.

"But it's so cheap. And then there's the baby."

"If you don't bargain she'll feel bad, figure she made the price too low. Then she'll kick herself all the way home, wondering what she could have gotten."

Ernie unearths two long dresses at a dollar each. One is Mexican, white with tiny eyelets, the other from India, pale purple with little mirrors.

I have a sudden insight.

"All these things we're buying have been worn."

"Well, of course they have, little one. How else did you explain the prices to yourself?"

"I thought they were without sales tax or something. Like when we used to go shopping across the border in Buffalo and wear two or three sets of clothes home so we wouldn't get caught. I'm not sure wearing strangers' clothing is healthy, Ernie."

"Nothing that's fun is healthy. Now I'm going to get you three blouses to wear with your very own jeans and then we'll be done."

From the back of a truck, painted with a scene of the Crucifixion, Ernie picks three soft silks: egg-white, mauve and silver-gray, together costing ten dollars.

"Ernie, exactly what kind of image are you working on for me?"

He looks offended.

"Darling, I'm absolutely not working on an image. I'm attempting to capture and express vibrations that emanate from you. Specifically your restrained sexuality: muted, subtle, a little old-fashioned."

"Like the Queen Mother?"

"Snow, I don't think you mean that as a complimentary comparison, am I right?"

He leads me with my packages to rest on washing machine and refrigerator parts.

"If you mean, do I see you as uptight, prune faced, rigid, proud-that-I'm-a-virgin, you're wrong. You're soft and naughty in a non-blatant way. That means sexy."

"Not frigid?"

"Au contraire, Snow. Always ready to be awakened, again and again."

We pretend to look at an old Westinghouse fridge.

"Now, Snow, how do you like your new clothes?"

"They're beautiful. Can I treat you to a drink somewhere? You deserve it for putting up with me."

We drive to a greasy spoon and order cokes.

"Now let's talk about love."

So I tell him about Langley, doing my best to sound sophisticated, feet on the ground, the right note of cynicism in my voice.

"You're in way over your head, aren't you?"

"Ernie, you're not supposed to see that. I gave you a cold, factual presentation of events."

"Sure."

"Is that all you're going to say? I need to know what you think. Am I acting like an idiot? Why didn't he sleep with me? You think he took me out to dinner figuring I'd be an easy lay and then got bored with me? You think he went home and told his wife amusing anecdotes about the new kid at work? Maybe I'm an experimental factor in a research report he's writing for the parent company back east? Or perhaps he's recruiting for the C.I.A. and I failed the initial test?"

"Whoa. Hold on, Snow. If I'm still allowed to be in this conversation, then let me answer. And my answer to all of the above is no. No, I don't think the guy is running a game on you. I think he's honestly attracted by an attractive woman. I've been trying to tell you you're a turn-on since the day we met at Macy's."

I must have given Ernie a funny look.

"What, you think because I prefer getting hard-ons around men that I don't know what a good-looking woman is? Don't be a bigot, Snow."

"Sorry."

"Your Langley sounds lovely, a little confused maybe, but real. A good experience. Pity he's a hetero." Ernie sighs.

"What about his being married?"

"Ah, yes. Well, to tell you the truth, I'm involved in something similar myself."

I choke on my coke.

"Snow, the rules you grew up with just aren't applicable anymore. Married, straight, gay, age, class, country, profession. Assume nothing and start from there. Is your partner gentle with you? Is he honest? Do you feel good with him? That's about all there is, honey."

"And what about you, Ernie? Is it good for you?"

Something goes sad in his face, like a small evening wave rippling over the beach.

"Oh, you know the syndrome. Like everybody else, I just want to live happily ever after. But nobody knows what that means anymore. I love him and I miss him when he's not with me. I get incredible spasms of jealousy and make scenes, the whole crummy story. But, honey, don't listen to Phase D right now when you're just entering Phase A. Phase A's the time for dreaming and fun. Come on, chicken. I'll take you home."

"Ernie, do you think if you felt down and wanted a shoulder you'd call me?"

"Sure."

And I believe him.

CHAPTER 15

At the GROWTH morning meeting, Langley avoids my eyes as he snake charms us into readiness to coil and spring at our day's victim. The quiet, sweet melody of his voice cloaks the inner dagger of steel that prods us down whatever road he chooses. We don't resist. There's no logical reason to; it all feels so good.

I search for the small, unsure boy who took me to dinner. He's gone to his room, but I catch him peeking out shyly in the pauses between words, thinking that he isn't seen. I wish he would wink at me, just to say hello, but if he sees me, he pretends not to. It's as if our evening together has been unthunk, never existed.

I pick up my briefcase, ready to follow Bridget to the car, shielding my eyes from Franny's and her question marks. I walk quickly by the podium area. He owes me nothing. I have no claims on him and don't wish to pressure. The main thing now is to hold onto some dignity, not to show how naive I was, building childish expectations after one silly date. The man was a little bored that day and thought it might be mutually pleasant to spend some time together. That's all. A hand touches my shoulder.

"Snow, I'd like to see you in the office when you get back today. Is that possible?"

"Sure."

I turn my head, but he's already gone. What does this mean? That Ernie was right, that he does care about me? But a small fist clamps shut in my stomach, refusing to let in that possibility. In the car I write a scenario in keeping with the bleaker fantasy: Snow, I just want to apologize for the other night. It wasn't fair to involve you in a personal crisis. Let's pretend it didn't happen, okay?

It's my first work day in a black neighborhood, and though I've learned to say black and not Negro, I still feel like the first European explorer reaching Africa, surrounded by the unknown, in the Dark Continent. The suburb is like any other at this hour, a world of women and pre-school children, television, washing machines and telephones. But the darkness of the skin behind the familiar activities causes an imbalance in my brain. The only blacks I've known are on television, rioting, or marching or being otherwise oppressed. I have no categories for doing dishes and changing diapers.

"Hello, I've been asked to call on mothers in the area."

The words suddenly ring differently when I think of a black mother and her children. How does she feel when she looks at these books I'm selling, full of pictures of white people? As black faces peer out doorways, I begin to stumble over my introduction, and the faces withdraw. Langley and company didn't prepare me for this, and the small, suspicious fist in my gut clamps itself shut, tighter than before.

Finally, a middle-aged woman takes pity on me and lets me into her home. I make my way into a negative print of familiar territory: black baby in playpen, black toddler in front of television and black woman patting a space for me beside her on the couch. She waits patiently for me to begin my spiel. I can't.

"Now you said you were here to talk to mothers. I sure qualify. I've got eight. Are you sure you're okay, hon?"

"Could I have a glass of water?"

"How about a cup of coffee?" She looks very concerned.

"I'd love one," and I try to sound reassuring.

I watch the Captain and Mr. Greenjeans with the toddler. Is he as unaware as I was that all the people on the TV are white? Does he identify more with the many-colored puppets? No sale is going to result from letting my mind wander like this, so I call it back to order and will myself to focus on the task at hand.

By the time the mother brings a small tray with two cups of coffee, sugar, milk and arrowroot biscuits, I'm in control again. I take a sip of coffee, focus on her eyes which are like anybody else's, and begin.

"As I said, I'm calling on mothers in this area. Before I go any further I'll ask a few questions to make sure you qualify for our new pre-school education program."

She follows with the required nod and continues giving appropriate responses to my questions. However, when we reach the matter of husband's employment, she answers that they live on welfare. At this point, according to the script, I am to fill in the correct box, thank her for the coffee, tell her someone may be in touch, and get the hell out as fast as I can to find a neighbor with a working husband. Instead, I sit, sip some more coffee and wonder what it's like to be black and out of work.

"That must be hard with eight kids."

"We manage," she smiles. "What with food stamps and all, it's not too bad. I do worry about the kids getting good schooling, though. That's why I was interested in what you might be offering for children."

She waits expectantly for me to go on and I'm embarrassed.

"What are food stamps?"

"You're not from around here, are you? They're coupons to buy food. The government gives them out. It's just like money at any supermarket as long as you buy food, not liquor or cigarettes. I get them every month from my welfare worker. Couldn't manage without. Where you from, honey?"

"Canada. I'm new at this job."

"Well, what is it you're here for? If you're selling, I'm willing to listen. You can get on with it."

She settles back into the cushions, warm and comforting. Being near her is relaxing my stomach. I figure I owe her honesty.

"I'm selling a program for kids: books, tapes, records. But the whole thing is on a payment plan and the credit company we work with won't accept the order if nobody in the family is working."

"I understand. Won't hurt to have a look at what they got, though."

With no pressure to sell or follow the script, I show her everything, pausing for questions, asking her opinions on the material. By the third cup of coffee, she's telling me the story of her marriage at sixteen and how she didn't finish high school. By pickup time, she's shared with me her dreams for each of the eight children and has begun to urge me to finish university.

"It's not too late for you either," I say, picking up my kit. If I'm really helping to liberate this woman, I need to be encouraging her to go to school herself, not to stay home helping her kids.

She smiles. "Naw, my chance is over. But it'll be fun watching the little ones. You take care now."

I go wait for the car; my insides are calmer, but my thoughts are more confused than before. That woman herself agrees with Langley: that her step to independence is through helping her kids. So who am I to judge? Why can't I follow the instructions of those who know better than I do? I wasted a whole day gabbing, deliberately not reaching my goal, investing energy in what Langley calls a no-win situation. Shame creeps over me.

As we ride back to the office I begin to feel frightened again. This time it's not a fist but a vibrating, onion-thin membrane. I can't trust myself. I'm on a blind road to self-destruction and the worst of it is the humiliation. My ignorance reduces me to no one, nothing, to discovering I'm manipulated with no will of my own. If I'm to be cast in the role of unknowing victim, at least let the Nazis shoot me while I'm trying to escape. I don't want to file in an orderly line to the gas chamber, unclothed and betrayed. I don't want to be prodded into a cattle car to die in my own piss with the rest of the cargo.

I knock at Langley's door.

"You want to see me?"

"Please. Come in and shut the door."

I sit down, trembling, clutching my briefcase, and remain frozen, listening, as he locks the door. He doesn't move closer.

"Don't be scared, Snow. You're shaking. I won't hurt you. Please put your case down. I won't touch you, even come near you, unless you say it's okay." He pauses. "Is it okay?"

I'm shaking so hard I don't know if I mean to nod my head or not, but Langley takes it as a yes. He crosses, picks me up in his arms and holds me to him, covering me with kisses. I can't hold on anymore and burst out crying. He pauses, feeling my tears, and then gently licks them from my cheeks, saying, "Baby, my baby." I can't stand on my feet now and begin to crumble, trying to keep my balance, sinking with Langley onto my knees. He doesn't let go but guides me until we're lying on the carpet. I've become nothing but sensations, a lightning rod conducting electrical impulses. I lie quivering as he caresses my body, his hand gliding over clothing, never touching skin, preserving that boundary as protection. He touches surfaces: imprinting, memorizing contours.

His mouth touches eyes, lips and ears, exploring my face with greater intimacy. My hands reach to stroke his head and at my slight movement, he shudders and stretches his weight on top of me. I feel him hard against my pelvic bone, pressing, waiting to explode. My body, no longer under control of my brain, pushes, my back arching and releasing. Langley supports his weight with his arms, circles and matches his rhythm to mine until he cries out, holding himself still and pulsating against me. Tears still streaming down my face, I hold him.

After a while the crying stops and he moves his head to look at me. I look back and smile.

"God, you're marvelous," he says, shifting his weight from me. "I'm sorry it happened this way, though. It's just that your openness, your vulnerability, is such a turn-on. I didn't mean to get carried away like that." He laughs. "That sounds ridiculous, doesn't it?"

"Yeah, sort of."

He touches my hair.

"You're so soft. Imagine what it'll be like making love for real. I want to gather you up, take all your clothes off, tuck you next to my skin under my jacket and keep you there forever. However, right now I'm going to freshen up and then make us a cup of coffee."

I straighten my clothes. Thought processes still haven't returned. I push myself against the wall, sitting on the carpet. I am in this room with no connection to past or future. My body still pulsates to some weird beat that isn't its own. I watch Langley pour from his Mr. Coffee machine and hand me a steaming cup.

"Snow, I guess I'm probably a little bit crazy."

He bends to sit beside me and pulls out a package of Dunhill cigarettes.

"Do you like to smoke after love-making?"

He lights one for me and I take little puffs so as not to throw up from the strong tobacco.

"You're in my head too often. When I touched you today, I couldn't let go of you. I don't understand it myself and I surely don't expect you to."

"Langley, you don't even know who I am."

"I know that. But I still feel the way I do. And I also feel you know me better than anyone else in the world does, as if you're my closest friend. Pretty strange, huh?"

Thoughts run through my head. He doesn't look like he's lying or making fun of me. There's no logical reason for him to play games with me. I'm obviously willing to be with him, so he doesn't have to seduce me. And if it's all a joke, why would he invest this much energy? I need to trust somebody. After my experience today with the black mother, I certainly can't trust myself. How would Langley react if I told him the Nazis were back? Would he be disappointed that his power hadn't worked and so move on to more fertile ground? Maybe he's just nuts.

"You don't trust me, do you?"

"No."

"And you're frightened."

"Yes. I'm afraid you're going to disappear, Langley. Like a genie who's given me my wish and now is getting ready to go back to his bottle. It just doesn't pay to get too attached to a genie."

He looks at me and breaks into the widest grin I've seen on him.

"Snow, I knew you were a very remarkable person, but it's still a delight to be surprised by you. When am I going to see you again?"

"Tomorrow morning, Langley, at the meeting."

"You know I don't mean that. Shall we go to a movie?"

"Sure."

I have one hand on the doorknob, with not enough strength to open the door and go. I stare at the carpet where we've been. It looks the same as the rest of the carpet.

"Next Monday night?"

"Yes."

"You'd better go now or I'll be pulling you back down on the rug."

I leave.

The walk home is incredible. I can actually feel the cosmos: all the stars and all their planets, each planet forever orbiting its predestined pattern around its sun. I am part of this Universe, part of this plan. If it's true. If I can believe Langley really sees me and knows me as his complement, his soul partner, then my life has meaning. Then I am following my path as it was meant to be. I finally understand what "star-crossed lovers" means. And it won't matter if I die at the end of the fifth act because I will be following my destiny and I will have fulfilled my purpose. I vibrate with the emanations of the galaxies.

In the apartment Taye is smoking and listening to "Mr. Tambourine Man." My face must be shining.

"Are you in love, Snow?"

"I guess so."

"It's not worth it." She pauses. "That's a lousy thing to say, isn't it? So cancel it. Enjoy yourself. That's what I want to say. Enjoy yourself."

I leave her smoking and start towards the bedroom.

"Snow, don't forget. This weekend is the annual women's camping trip."

"The what?"

"Camping. Women. We leave Friday after work and we'll be back on Sunday evening. I have an extra sleeping bag, if you need it. I signed you up to bring Fritos and other salty things."

I look at Taye curled on a cushion, smoking, eyes closed, and I know that she too has her place in the universe. I forgive her for her mundane talk of salty things.

CHAPTER 16

*T*he car ride to the camp-
ground in Novarro is not fun. Taye sits in the front, talking
excitedly with one of her friends from her group and I'm
crowded in the back seat between two others. It's cramped
and hot and I feel unwanted, the extra sardine in the can.
Taye has only invited me out of a mixture of pity and duty. I
should have stayed home and done hand laundry.

As we travel north, the weather gets warmer and stickier
and I can glimpse farm country over the heads of the others,
each of them with her window position. I feel sick to my
stomach.

The talk is all about their group and their leader Nancy.
Does Nancy's affair with Dalia, another group member,
affect her judgment in working with the other group mem-
bers? Taye is the most vocal.

"Nancy has a right to have an affair with whoever she
wants. What worries me is that her energy is caught up in
that relationship. I also have a right, as does each group
member, to Nancy's objective intervention, not to mention
her special attention and love."

They scare me with their talk of rights. Who's deciding

what and for whom? The thought of a lesbian couple scares me. How do they act together? How do I act towards them?

We enter a forest of giant redwoods. The smell of the trees, spicier than that of Muskoka, fills the car. As we penetrate the forest, the talk grows more sporadic and finally is awed into stillness by the immensity of the place. We reach a side road and follow it to a clearing with tents unfurled under trees. The car engine turned off, the first sound is of a river. I help unload our gear, enjoying the dominance of forest and water over the human. Words, opinions, relationships are dwarfed by the touch of dried leaves, twigs and soft earth under my feet.

"Lots of good firewood," says somebody.

"Come on, Snow," says Taye, "I'll take you for a quick stroll before the others get here and we start organizing things."

I feel a rush of gratitude at her gesture to be with me.

"You feel kind of out of it, don't you? I'm not going to baby you, though. It won't take long. They're all good people."

We scout out the area. Small groups have separated themselves by distance and trees to create total privacy. Each group has two basics: a fire space ringed by stones, and a tent, the quality of which ranges from blanket to pre-fab geodesic dome. A couple of the areas are really developed. One has a lean-to kitchen, utensils and pots hanging from wooden pegs. A family has built swings and a tree-house.

"Some people come for the whole summer. Around that bend is a witch with a root cellar and a herb garden. You can buy things from her."

The campers smile and greet us. Like with Franny in Berkeley, no one intrudes, but at the same time there is an invitation to join or an offer of help, if needed. Boundaries can be blurred. It's safe. After all, we'll all eventually be going back to the city.

We reach the river. It's clear: at the shoreline, fast running over rocks, further out, deepening into quiet pools. The movement delights me: not the lake and not the ocean, water moving with a plan of its own. I stretch my arms to catch the last rays of the afternoon sun. Behind us the campground is loose, without structure; nothing has been organized in advance, not even a public toilet.

"Taye, how do you go to the bathroom?"

"In the woods. Cover it with earth and bring the paper back to the campsite to burn. Leave the place like you found it. This is our third year here and I've never seen it dirty."

We move back to the other women and set up our site: tents with soft grass inside for sleeping bags, a pit for the fire, a kitchen area with cartons of food set on rocks. I'm appointed to gather dry firewood and move off to fulfill my task. I've been scooped up into an orchestra, given sheet music and trusted to play my part. Everybody knows the symphony: when to solo, play in duet, join the chorus. There's no conductor, the work just gets done.

I've never seen such coordination of effort without someone barking out orders. There's hardly any talking. Roles aren't defined; the knowing is intuitive. The women are organizing for and by themselves. No man is involved in the getting or the giving. Is this what accounts for the absence of rigidity and the lack of egos crashing?

I've been around women, bathrooms and gym classes and stuff. I've played with just girls as a kid. But I've never contemplated anything serious without a male component, even if it was only to anticipate male criticism or approval. Women's groups, as far as I'm concerned, are social groups for people who can't find a mate. This female working unit

142

that has enfolded me now threatens basic concepts. I wish there was some guy here to balance things.

The air is turning chilly and Taye takes me under her wing to our tent. We spread out our sleeping bags and arrange the space with the two other women, Martha and Ceely, who are sleeping with us. We change to long pants and sweaters and I try not to stare.

"You're Taye's roommate, aren't you?"

I have to look at her. Martha has large, full breasts. I make my eyes keep moving to her face.

"Taye's told us about you."

To my relief, she pulls on her sweater.

We rub on mosquito lotion and join the others to prepare dinner. The working tempo has accelerated. Now a jazz band, we simmer a stew on a tripod, bake potatoes wrapped in tinfoil on the coals, and cut vegetables for the salad. Total concentration is on the activity, each involved in her job, we are part of the larger whole. I'm almost free of wondering who I am. Is this what it's like to be a man?

In the gathering darkness there is only an occasional soft sentence. I hear Nancy's name called and see her turn, a graceful woman in her early forties, hair pulled back in a graying braid, eyes with crinkle lines lit by the fire.

The delicious smell of the stew grows unbearable. It's pitch black by the time we sit around the fire to eat, mopping up gravy with chunks of homemade bread. Taye has left me on my own, and mellowed by food, I decide to risk conversation.

"I'm Snow. A friend of Taye's."

"I'm Gerry."

She doesn't turn and all I can see is a hard profile under a short-cropped head.

"So, what do you do when you're not camping?"

"If you mean for money, I'm an electrician."

She takes a bite of bread, chews it slowly and turns to fix me with a cold stare.

"But I'm political. That's what I do. I work with my sisters. Do you?"

"No. Not really."

"Well, you know what they say, if you're not for us, you're against us."

Dismissing me, she returns concentration to her food.

I join a contingent washing dishes with soapless soap in the river and return with my work crew to the fire, away from Gerry. I'm beginning to forget her and enjoy biting into a S'more – a graham cracker, chocolate and marshmallow sandwich melted over the fire – when I'm horrified to see Langley's face dancing in the flames. Gerry is right. I'm betraying them all. I try to exorcise the image, but with no success. It only gets worse as I feel his lips exploring me, his voice in my ear. I am corrupted. I bury my shame in my arms.

Crawling humiliated into my sleeping bag, I invite my old night-time pal, Free, to come into my dreams. He arrives with his band of guerrillas, but all the fun is gone. I'm no longer inside that body, the object of their animal desires. I stay an outsider watching, wondering what is wrong with that girl who dreams.

I wake in the morning to a terrible sense of loss and the smell of frying bacon. The sun is streaming through the open tent flap and I'm alone inside. Pulling on bathing suit and T-shirt, I walk out into the brilliant light pouring through the trees, the chirping of birds and breakfast talk.

"Hey, Snow," calls Nancy, her hair copper red in the morning light. "About time you woke up. Come and eat before it's all cold."

I approach and take the proffered plate.

"You okay? I noticed Gerry giving you a hard time last night."

I fill the plate with scrambled eggs, bacon and a toasted bagel with cream cheese. Nancy hands me coffee and motions for me to sit by her. I feel no pressure to talk; I eat and feel the fresh air lifting the hair on my neck and the sun-warmed rock beneath me. There's a gentleness about Nancy that removes the threat of knowing she's a lesbian. I don't feel demands from her, sexual or otherwise. If I wanted to, I could tell her anything, and she would listen and not judge. She's about the same age as my mother, yet instead of threatened, I feel safe.

I'm free to check out the rest of the women without danger of attack. A slender brunette sits down next to us and is introduced as Dalia. I remember she's Nancy's lover. There is a specialness between them and I feel shy, wondering if I should move away. But they share a smile with me and the three of us sip our coffee.

Somebody shouts, "Let's go swimming," and there's a rush for the river. By the time I reach the water, everybody is naked except for me.

"Snow, don't be silly," shouts Taye. "Take off your bathing suit. Nobody's looking. All the campers here are cool. Straight people don't know about this place."

I breathe deeply for courage and peel off my suit. The sun coats my body, breasts surprised and welcoming. My tent-mate, Martha, takes my hand as I navigate the rocks into the cold river water. The current grabs us and I tumble into the stream, my nakedness embraced by the thrusting rapids. I laugh aloud and faces smile back. We drift downriver, finding rocks to perch on or hang onto, lying on sandy places. We splash and shout at each other, and I gradually relax and let myself enjoy the beauty of the water nymphs. Once, for a few minutes lying cupped in a shallow place, I find myself beautiful too.

Wrapped in towels, we eat lunch at our campsite, in the shade of the trees. It's a feast of salads: crab, avocado, fruit, vegetable, and huge glasses of iced tea. They talk about projects for the coming year: work with a black women's group, escorting rape victims through trial procedure.

"Speaking of rape," says Dalia, "my ex is in town and is hassling me again about getting custody of the kids."

She starts to cry and Nancy puts a protective arm around her. I'm jealous.

After lunch the women split into groups, to swim, play backgammon, nap. I read my James Bond book, waiting to get caught.

"Well, if it isn't Snow, one of our weekend political parasites."

It's Gerry, the electrician. I welcome her words. It's so much easier having someone else say them than listening to my own voice.

"What do you mean, Gerry?"

"You feed off the women's movement, getting the perks, equal opportunities for all, without putting anything on the line yourself."

"That's probably true."

"You sound proud of it. I had a feeling about you even before we met. The kind that makes a plan with a girlfriend on condition she doesn't get asked out by a man."

"But everybody does that."

"Not anymore they don't. Some women no longer feed off other women's pain and struggle. Some women have given up the role of passive, consenting slug: perfect victim, born partner to some pig man's ego."

I excuse myself and go to the tent to doze. Pictures of Amazon women, breast bared and arrows ready, intersperse themselves with images of 007. Who is the prey? Is it me? Am I the enemy? By my compliance, by my silence, on this level too I've joined the ranks of those who "didn't know" the gas chambers were there. I am of the same flesh as those who named names to the McCarthy Committee, the less than human beings. I have become that image from my childhood, equated with evil incarnate. But why does Gerry blame me so? I am, after all, merely a superfluous waste product.

In the late afternoon a few of us hike along a trail through the forest. The sky is fearless blue and the redwoods warm from the sun. I feel comfortable in the silence, accepted by the hikers. It takes a long time to prepare dinner. Whole chickens are trussed on spits over fire pits. We take turns turning them as the sun sets and dark takes over. I bring out the salty things and get appreciative murmurs. The coals glow and spark from the dripping chicken fat. Taye starts a joint, Nancy produces wine, and we sink cozily into blurred edges until the chicken's pronounced done and we can eat. I look around at the firelit faces and I know I've known them forever: chemical elements, parts of myself, binding through water and fire, earth and air. I can travel inside each one's head and I suddenly realize they must be able to tour around inside me too. I can feel them there. It tickles and I start to giggle. I can't stop. I try to control it, but others around me have started too.

When we finally come to a gasping halt, I feel I owe them an explanation.

"I've never felt like this before. So close to so many at one time. I didn't know I could. Like something inside me was closed and now it's open."

They laugh and nod, welcoming me into a club. Even Gerry looks hopeful. Nancy reaches over and squeezes my hand.

"Taye, I'm really glad I came," I say on the way to the tent.

"Don't mention it, kid."

I do not dream of Langley.

In the morning most of the other women make some move to introduce themselves.

"I'm Shirley. I got very fond of you last night, Snow. Thought I'd get to know you better."

"Pat. Mother of two. Active in Fat Lib."

"My name's Cyd. I'm pretty new here too."

At the river we sunbathe, smoothing on baby oil, brushing each other's hair. Taye catches me with tears.

"Why can't it stay like this?"

"It just never does. We talk about it sometimes, but I think we'd just get bored. Besides, each of us has got her own particular shtick in the city and we're each too independent to give that up. But it sure is good for the batteries, is it not?"

Gerry finds me while we're packing to go.

"I want you to know that I realize you're struggling."

She turns as abruptly as she spoke, leaving me with no shred of definable defense from the intensity of the weekend.

CHAPTER 17

*T*he camping trip leaves me with a dream. I am the Nile: sun drenched, winding my way through the Fertile Crescent, the Source of all life, deep beyond imagination, without beginning or end. I flow through Time, indestructible, yet my banks are soft and yielding. My river bed seeks rest above the earth's fiery core while my surfaces lie open and churning to the temptations of the universe. I am truly alone, forever content in my own currents and undulations.

At least until the blast of the atomic bomb.

Still half dreaming, and coated with Solarcaine, I return to work and wind my way door to door, on automatic pilot, selling all the world's knowledge on the installment plan, distributing the little tin box with the happy face to women with dead eyes in ranch-style houses. Their lives end in a carpeted box. Don't they know about the river?

"You look like a lobster," says Franny. "Where've you been?"

"I went camping. I'm sorry I haven't called you to thank you for my Berkeley visit. I'd like you to come stay at my place too. I'll call. We'll make a plan."

I try to move away from her.

"No sweat, Snow. Speaking of sweat, I've joined a gym and started going to Weight Watchers. I've lost five pounds. When I reach twenty, I'll call my parents."

"That's great, Franny."

"You can eat everything but junk on their diet as long as it's the right amounts. We have meetings once a week, like Langley's, but not as sexy. I'm really feeling good. Let me tell you what I ate today. You won't believe it."

"Franny, I really want to hear. But later, I've got to run."

She looks crushed. I give her a hug, but she pulls away.

"Hey, I'm all right. What's with this touchy, feely stuff? Don't tell me you're going gay on us."

"Sorry. Just felt close to you. Like a sister. I'll catch you later."

"Whatever."

I imagine Gerry's analysis of this conversation, especially now, as I duck into the bathroom to hide from Franny so she won't see me going into Langley's office.

But my doubts are pushed aside as Langley locks the door and takes me into his arms. The camping trip fades. I even forget my sunburn as I concentrate on his mouth seeking mine. Nothing can be more important than these signals my body is sending me, telling me I'm home now, I can take off my armor, stretch out in front of the castle fire and know that the enemy will stay beyond the moat. We pull away, panting and grinning.

"Langley, I'm starting to believe this is really happening."

"I'll pick you up at eight for the film."

He takes me to Woody Allen's *Bananas*, which I've already seen but I act like it's the first time so as not to cause embarrassment. We sit in the dark of the back row, faces pointed towards the screen. Langley's fingers gently open my blouse and stroke my stiffened nipples. He teases, touching me to excitement, until I want to crush his mouth onto my breasts, his body into mine. But I sit quietly, hands gripping the arm rests, eyes on the South American revolution as brought to us by Howard Cosell.

I can't help letting out a small sigh and Langley chuckles. He pulls my fingers towards him, to his coat-covered lap, to opened fly and hardened penis. He guides me, stroking, closing his hand over mine. I let him, owing comfort in return for the attention he has given me. He moans, and he and my hand are showered and then lie limp together on his thigh. I await direction. He leans over and kisses me on the cheek.

"Thank you."

He cleans us with a handkerchief, and gently holding hands, we watch the film. When the lights come up, it's as though nothing has happened.

"Have you been to the top of the new Hyatt Regency?"

I shake my head no. We drive through the crowded streets. He talks about the film and the genius of Woody Allen. Is he assuming a sexual sophistication on my part, that I'm used to these encounters, or does he just not care?

The new hotel is intimidating with its elegant lobby, marquee-lit elevators and smooth-as-glass waterfall. I feel like everyone is staring at my sperm-stained hand and it seems to swell under their scrutiny. I mumble excuses and run for the bathroom, straight to the sink, to scrub it clean.

I'm alone in the plushness of pinks and reds and giant mirrors. With my clean hands, I sit down at the makeup table and stare in the gilt-framed mirror at the flushed face staring back. The face is prettier than I remember it. I was afraid I'd look coarsened and hag-like, but I look vital and alive. I brush my hair and fix my makeup. I only wish I could stay in the safety of this room forever. Two other women enter, talking softly, respecting my privacy, taking their own.

But still I feel exposed and stand to leave. The girl in the full-length mirror watches me: dark-gray pants and silver-gray blouse, dark eyes shining. One need not be ashamed to be with her. I go out to the lobby.

Langley rests in an armchair. He doesn't see me. His head is cupped in his hand, his face tired and a little sad. He feels me looking at him and his face lights up as he comes towards me.

"I thought I'd lost you, scared you off in the movie. Please don't just disappear. Tell me if something's wrong. You promise?"

I nod, feeling high and in control. We rise in the elevator, peering out the glass walls at the people below, Langley's arm delicately around my shoulder, and exit into dim light and an upholstered tunnel. He guides me through, my eyes adjusting to the darkness. I'm prepared for a surprise but still gasp as we are spilled out at the entrance to a revolving restaurant, tables and chairs moving slowly by the San Francisco skyline.

"I thought you'd like it, Snow," and he kisses the top of my head.

We mount the carousel and I watch the city wave to me as we circle by. Langley leads me to a free table.

"What are those wads of paper stuck under the window frames?"

"Take one and open it."

I pull out a crumpled ball and read, "Hey, you gorgeous thing at Table 6. Ditch that creep and meet me outside at 12:30." I put the paper back as our table passes the next window frame. Our movie house gropings now seem more in context.

"What will you drink?"

"Bloody Mary."

He orders a Jack Daniels for himself. I'd like to tell him

about myself, but it seems like information might spoil something. He's already decided who I am and anything that contradicts his concept threatens to destroy. Where there are words there is danger. I need to learn to bask in his eyes bathing mine, and not to question. I'm rewarded for my silence.

"How lucky we are to have found each other," he says. "You know what I'd like to do? I'd like to be on some deserted island, just the two of us, and touch and," he laughs, "touch some more. I want to explore every tiny part and crevice of your body."

I look down to hide my blushing. The vodka is blurring my brain edges. I'm beginning to believe the girl in the mirror. He must want more than sex because if that was all he wanted he could have been in and out of my body a long time ago. There must be something about me other than the holes that he sees. He keeps saying I'm somebody he doesn't want to lose.

"Langley, I'm confused. You don't really know me. What is it you see? When I'm with you I don't ask these questions, but afterwards I try to figure it all out. You talk as if you almost love me, like you wanted us to be a couple, make promises to each other."

Langley signals the waitress for another round. I turn to watch the lights flicker by outside to give him time to answer. The drink comes and he sips his whiskey.

"Snow, you're a real worrier, aren't you? Neither of us knows what will be. The only question is, do we feel good together? I do. Every moment is precious. I can say what I feel, and I do. I don't want to ruin it with analyses, hows and whys. What we have now is only an embryo of something. We have to nurture it and see what it grows into, not kill it with all our questions and fears. Why are you so frightened?"

"I'm starting to care for you. Maybe expect things."

153

"Ah, expectations. They'll kill us all."

"And when I'm not with you I get worried you're making fun of me, like it's a game for you. I imagine you at your squash club, telling the fellas about the new girl at work and how she fell for a snow job. You're good at selling things, you know."

"But I don't belong to a squash club. Hey, Snow, that's a joke."

"I think you'd better take me home now."

"If that's what you want, Snow."

We start to get up. He looks at me with such concern that I wonder if I'm about to have a heart attack.

"Why are you looking at me like that?"

"Like what?"

"Like you need to call an ambulance."

"I'm deciding what to do here. Okay, I've decided. Snow, sit down. Just a few more minutes. I've decided not to let you walk out of my life quite so fast. I've been thinking too much about myself and too little about you. I didn't realize how little self-confidence you have. I thought with your sales record you must be bursting with self-worth. Now I see my coming on so strong must scare you. You're trembling, aren't you?"

"Is that why you made a joke of it? Made fun of me?"

"Yes. And I guess I was hurt that you thought I was a locker-room type. It took me a while to realize you were putting yourself down and not me. Dirty jokes at the squash club indeed! I'm far from perfect, but I'm not the kind that hangs out telling smutty stories."

A tear runs down my cheek and Langley wipes it away.

"You're very precious, special. You need to learn who you are. I'd like to help you, not hurt you. That doesn't mean there might not be pain sometime for both of us. Then we weigh it up, balancing the good with the bad, and decide. Right now for me it's good."

"What about your wife?" I immediately wish I could cancel my mundane question, but he answers without taking offense.

"I have a wife and I have two children, whom I love very much. I try to be honest with myself and at the same time not cause them unnecessary suffering. She's very jealous and I protect her from knowing hurtful things. I lie to her, Snow. Do you hate me for it?"

"No. You know I don't hate you. But I don't know if you're lying to me."

"I don't lie about my feelings, Snow."

A wave of exhaustion sweeps over me, my circuits are overloaded. Why can't I just say "Hurray" and have a good time?

"Snow! What a glorious surprise. And to think I almost missed you."

I look up into Ernie's grinning face and he winks. His companion is a slighter and younger man.

"You look radiant. Aren't you going to introduce me to your friend?"

Both Langley and Ernie's friend Seaton scowl, but we make the introductions.

"We're on our way out. I'll call you."

Ernie kisses my hand and guides Seaton to the exit.

"Who's that?" Langley is still scowling.

"He's my friend. And I do believe you're jealous."

"So?"

"It's lovely. You really do care about me."

He sighs.

"Okay, Langley. I've decided. I'll take a chance. No more doubts. From now on you and I are on the same side."

He smiles. "Will you go away with me next weekend? I have a cottage in Mendocino. I want to take you there."

"Sure. Of course I will. I'd love to."

"Well, that's settled then. You've made me very happy, do you know that? We can make definite plans during the week."

Langley threads his way through the tables, moving off the revolving platform towards the cash register. I watch women's heads turn to appreciate him and then glance questioningly at me. The wolves howl inside. I've chosen not to listen to them, the girl in the mirror says I don't need to. But for a moment I want to hurl myself through the window into the arms of the city below to avoid the humiliation. I hear their voices: What does he see in her? He's old enough to be her father. What does he need with an unsophisticated girl like that? What can she possibly offer him except you know what, and she's probably not very good at that either. Maybe it's a charity case. She's somebody's cousin.

I know I'm naive and easy to fool, that my ideas of a love affair come from books and movies. I need to grow up, act like an adult, take responsibility. I know that Langley doesn't want a serious relationship with me. The man is married. He uses words like love, but for him love is something for the moment. He goes through dozens like me. Knowing this, it's my decision, my choice, whether to let him add me to his list.

"What's wrong, Snow?" He holds me, descending in the glass elevator.

"Nothing. I'll miss you until next weekend."

He squeezes me to him. So what! I'm an easy lay. There, I've defined myself, and feel better already. I'm not a goody-goody anymore. I've joined the ranks of the high school scum bags. Besides, he's probably an excellent lover and

156

will teach me things for perpetuity. Every other girl at GROWTH would give her eye teeth to be in my position, that is if they already haven't. Why the hell should I pass up my golden opportunity for the sake of my parents' middle-class morals? He continues to whisper sweet nothings in my ear. Haven't I got as much right to hear sweet nothings as the next girl?

"Are you sure everything's okay?" he says in the car.

"Absolutely."

CHAPTER 18

"*T*here are those who get through life playing it safe, their cards kept close to the chest, never betting the whole kitty. And then there are the risk-takers."

Langley beams at the morning meeting.

"I've always been a risk-taker, and with all my heart, I highly recommend it."

Is he talking to me?

"Sure, we risk-takers get hurt on occasion, fail, fall in the mud. But seekers, when we take off and soar, we fly to heights that those poke-along, watch-out-and-be-careful folks can't even imagine. Life is too sweet not to be tasted, and if along the line we bite into a sour apple or two, we just need to know how to throw the rotten fruit under a bush and let it act as the good fertilizing agent it was meant to be, while you and I move on to sweeter pastures. And as for the good apples, we risk-takers know how to treasure, and cherish, and all those good things one does with tasty fruit."

He winks and a wave of giggles crosses the room. I hope I'm not blushing.

"We need to relearn how to take chances. We used to do

it a lot as kids. If at first you don't succeed etcetera, what's the worst that can happen? So we'll fall on our faces. No big deal, we'll pick ourselves up and move on. Right?"

He's right.

"Hey, seekers, I don't hear you. Am I right or am I right? We risk-takers pick ourselves up and move on. Right?"

"Right!" we thunder back.

In the field, feeling bad from parroting with the others, I keep up my personal sales talk. There's no way I could not have smiled and answered him. He's up there on the podium, needing support. If I sit silent I betray, so I conquer my repulsion at shouting in crowds and say I'm with him. Why refuse? All it gets me is a headache and loneliness in the stomach, for the sake of some principle. Why not believe and feel good? It's as simple as that. Stop looking for the catch, take a chance, feel good, and along the way sell some encyclopedias. You can't beat that.

I make my sale.

At home Taye teaches me to bake bread. The dough oozes around my fingers as I push and shape dry floury particles into sticky, and then sticky back to floury. Kneading, I am in control of the elements, changing form and shape according to my own plan and tempo, creating according to my whim. Life flows by my choice, through my fingers, and is accepted by the yeast and flour, who now can continue to grow without me. It's like impregnating a woman.

"I like your friends," I say to Taye, "especially Nancy."

"She liked you too. Said you ranked pretty high among the Snows."

I feel like I've been socked in the stomach. I had thought I'd been given special status, being invited to meet her women's group. Oh, cruel reality! But as Langley says, life goes on, and I continue to speak to her.

"You know, you talk to me like some kind of statistic."

"I know. It's self-protection."

She pushes her dough with all her strength.

"Snow, I explained to you at the beginning. We both know you're just passing through. I need to keep some distance, not get too attached, and especially not start feeling responsible. I have a tendency to mother things and get hurt too badly when they inevitably leave the nest. The group calls it trouble with boundaries. I don't keep track of where I end and where you begin."

"So why did you invite me on the camping trip?"

Taye laughs. "Now you see the problem."

She shows me how to bounce our lumps of dough into loaf-like forms and we place them to rise in bread pans covered with clean dish towels. Settled down to wait, with cups of ginseng tea, we watch the sun set behind Taye's loom through the living-room window. Her body as always is restless, one foot twitching, a hand twiddling a strand of hair. I know she has something more to say to me, but I don't ask. I'm learning to wait in silence, not fill up every space with words. The room grows darker.

"I'll tell you what's going on," she says after a long while. "It's only fair. I feel a warmth to you as a woman. Not sex, so don't get frightened. But close. And I know you're in the process of getting involved with some guy and I also know it's none of my business. But every bone in my body wants me to tell you to watch out. You're going to get used and abused. And I don't want you to expect me to pick up the pieces."

"Do you hate men, Taye?"

"No," she smiles. "I think they're often charming as company and they're certainly useful in bed. I, however, would not count on one of them for anything. For a friend I would only choose a woman."

"But women are the first to stab each other in the back." I try to sound satirical. "Women are catty, gossip mongers, insanely jealous, non-rational, emotionally unstable and petty."

"I know you're only half joking. I used to believe all that crap too in high school when we were being taught that's how it is. When I got married, I still believed it, and living in the suburbs didn't change things. The brain-washing process had already taken its toll on all of us. I was lucky, though. I didn't have kids, and I took courses at the university where I met women who'd broken out. They didn't need the lie anymore."

She pauses to check her watch.

"You and I better go see to the bread."

The dish towels are hugging soft, rounded forms. I watch Taye lift one warm mass onto the board and then begin to pound it with her fists, a savage grin on her face.

"This is my favorite part. I get all the people who've ever screwed me over lined up in my head, and I bash them in. This is for my mother, and this is for my father, and this is for my third-grade teacher who wouldn't let me go to the bathroom, and this is for the bastard who took my parking spot yesterday. Come on, Snow, join the fun."

"I haven't got them sorted out like you do. I wouldn't know where to start."

"It doesn't matter. Just say things like cock-sucker, fuck-face, prick, cunt."

"Prick," I pick the easiest and whack the dough. It's a surprisingly pleasing sensation.

"Thatta girl," encourages Taye. "Bastard!"

The board jumps under her flattened loaf.

"Mother-fucker," I try with more volume.

"Cunt, bitch," answers Taye.

We swear and bash with our fists until we both burst out

161

giggling, then remake the loaf shapes and put them back in the pans, undaunted to rise again. The living room is dark now. I light the corner lamp and collapse on the cushions. Taye brings ice cream, Baskin-Robbins Jamoca Almond Fudge. Seventy-five million calories ripple down my throat.

"His name is Langley."

"You've got to be kidding. Nobody's called Langley. He probably changed it from Marvin or something."

"Taye," I say, crunching a nut, "I will tell my story with dignity or not at all."

"All right. I'll be good."

But I hear her mutter Langley to herself as she takes another bite.

"I know it sounds like a soap opera, but I really don't want you to laugh anymore. He's my boss. All the girls are in love with him and, for whatever reasons, he's picked me to start up with. That's the hardest part for me to deal with. Why he sees me as the object of his affections. He doesn't know me. Except," I look to make sure she's not laughing, "sometimes it seems like we've known each other forever. And I think that's what love is. Not all the superficial information. He lets me in underneath all the big white leader trappings to see the scared little boy who wants to be cuddled and reassured. Is this making any sense?"

"All too familiar. Continue."

"It's two ways, though. He focuses on me too, senses changes and gives this kind of concentration that I've never felt before from anyone. I feel he's delighting in me, tasting who I am. He can't be lying because he reacts in the second that it's happening. It can't be planned. He must really care."

"You sound like you're trying to convince yourself."

It feels like she's making fun of me. I convince myself she isn't.

"But this isn't the first time something like this has

happened to me. I've been chosen before. At summer camp when I was fourteen there was a counselor who everybody thought was the epitome of manhood. He was nineteen. We dreamed about him, talked and made up stories. Near the end of the summer we all had personal interviews. I had mine with him in the camp truck. He chose me. And it didn't stop there. He wrote me beautiful letters and we saw each other for a long while. It was real. He wasn't using and abusing, Taye. Maybe I am special, magic, and not just another piece of meat to be chewed and swallowed. Maybe a man and I can love, and it's destined, has to be. Maybe Langley really needs me like he says he does. And I need him."

"Sort of like you validate each other, like you make the other exist. I've been there, Snow. It's a very dangerous place."

I concentrate on my ice cream and lie.

"So far he's taking more risks than I am, wanting reassurance that I won't disappear, telling me how important I am to him. Besides, he's married."

"Oh dear."

I can see her working at not saying whatever it is she wants to say. She reaches some sort of control.

"Look, I'm not going to preach to you, mainly because it won't work. You're an innocent and you'll just have to get your knocks like the rest of us. Why should I be the one to convince you there's evil in the world? You might just end up living happily ever after in your castle in the sky and prove me all wrong. I'd really like that, Snow. For it to be good for you. I don't want to be a bitter old woman at the age of twenty-five."

She starts to cry.

I don't know what to do except just sit and be silent. I wish I could get up and put my arms around her, but I can't.

She's the end of all the dreams that don't come true, and that scares me. I see rows of keening women dressed in black like those crones in *Zorba* who stoned the young widow. I feel pity for them. But if the choice is between crone and life, I don't want to be dragged into croneness. I'd rather be a mistress than a wife, if mistress means alive and loved and wife means dead and chained to duty. Better a chance with Langley than ruin in the safety of a uniformly designed plywood container in the suburbs. Taye would even agree with me on that.

"Sorry," she sniffles. "Things got out of hand. Would you do me a favor and check the bread?"

The loaves have again pushed their cloths into twin-breasted mounds. I call Taye into the kitchen.

"Okay, cookie," she sounds better, "now we bake. Give your loaf a little kiss good-bye and into the oven. Don't be scared, Snow. See, I'm all right. Really, I am."

"I'm not very used to seeing people cry. Except for myself, of course. I don't know what to do."

"You did fine. You let me be. Can't do anything better. It took me ages before I learned how to do that in group. You do it naturally. It's not hard to see what your Langley sees in you."

"Let's not go overboard with the compliments. Lest you get carried away, I suggest you have a talk with my mother, and she can fill you in on my true character. With her I am my real disgusting self."

"Whoa there, girl. I won't play that game with you. You can say thank you for the nice words, or you can tell me you don't like me. Whatever. But don't throw shit."

The smell of the baking bread begins to seep through the kitchen, covering us like a warm quilt.

"You're right, Taye."

She's found me out. I can't hear a simple compliment

164

without questioning the giver's sincerity. I have to throw it back in their face. But it just goes to show how disgusting I am, reinforcing the parasite-on-earth theory. People are dying in Vietnam and I'm caught up in the dilemma of whether Langley really loves me.

And yet who am I if no one loves me? I will be another nameless victim. The smell of the bread is lulling me, lullabying. We stare into our teacups.

"Should I join your women's group?"

"No," she answers softly. "You can't. You're too temporary, Snow. We're trying to build something: a community, a commitment."

"You're always talking about my leaving."

"The bread's ready. Let's take it out."

The loaves are golden and sweet smelling. We set them on the counter to cool and Taye takes out butter to soften for the morning. The breads have completed their task, manifested themselves, become who they are. Taye goes to bed, leaving me without her group and without Langley.

I am a particle of dust alone in space, pushed by air currents, without anchor and without goal. My only hope is to crash. Maybe then I might explode and disappear, not be condemned to drift forever without purpose or plan. All the others are in orbit, belonging to a system; they circle sources of energy that give sustenance and meaning to their existence. I could die and start over, born this time into a stellar scheme or at least a molecular function.

CHAPTER 19

*T*aye has disappeared, leaving a "need some distance" note on our untouched breads. I can't touch them without her; the feeling of utter loneliness, without a soul to care whether I live or die, is too strong. Logically, I'm sure that other people feel this way too; no reason to drag the body around, to clothe and feed it another day, but the thought offers no comfort. I'm bad for the ecology; my useless living is at someone else's expense. Someone who wants to live could use the extra food and clothing: a mother with dependent little kids, a poet almost finished his master work, a doctor volunteering his services in the jungles. If only it could be arranged for us parasites to die nobly; our sacrifice of direct benefit to those more worthy of life than we are.

As it is I contribute nothing, am only a source of pain and frustration to my family and to anyone else who gets involved with me. It doesn't take long for people to realize I am nothing and to move away, sensing the emptiness inside. Taye has gone. She is right about Langley, who hasn't said a word to me in private since our date. Franny, hurt by my rebuff, is avoiding me. I could call home, but that would signal total defeat, worse than death. I call Ernie but only his machine answers.

I have a cold, my face is caving into my head and dripping down into my chest cavity. Outside it's drizzling rain as I walk my encyclopedia route, the mothers transparent hologram figures, furniture and cracked toys visible through their bodies. They let me into their homes out of pity, listen to me whimper and shoo me out, hoping that a neighbor might be interested. As the day wears on, the walls of the houses writhe like crazy things and the street begins to coil, ready to spring.

At the GROWTH offices Langley's door is closed. There is no message. I run home, dripping and dripped on, to a cold apartment, morgue-like, waiting for a corpse to warm it. In the kitchen the bread is infested by ants swarming so thickly all I can see is black. I am nothing but a cheap feel in a movie theater, a fool deceived by charming words. How trite. Alack and alas. Woe is me!

How I wish I could drift off into some black void, as black as the ant pile, and that could be the end. If I could die in my sleep, without gas and without pills, taken away by some Force other than my own, my Prince Charming on a black horse, Death taking me in his arms and caressing me, lulling me to eternal peace, never to be born again. My throat hurts so badly I can barely swallow. I spray the ants and coldly watch them gasp to their final oblivion. Pity I don't have little ant crematoria to do the job properly.

My coat still on, I wander unbalanced and shaking from living room to kitchen to my bedroom and back again. Despite the cold, the apartment is suffocating. I need to get out, to feel the air on my face while I think of a non-messy way to die. If only Dorothy on her way home from Oz would splash a bucket of witch-melting water over my head. Outside it's dark and foggy. I head towards Van Ness,

167

lit with traffic and street lamps, where I won't get raped and distracted from dying. On the other hand, perhaps if I was raped and then killed, it might be worth it. Mother would have a new Cause, and father more reasons to feel sad and guilty.

Van Ness Avenue with its used-car lots further denies my existence, and I grow heavier and uglier as I walk until the weight is too much to bear. I sit on the curb, watching the rain water trickle in the gutter, envying its having a known destination. A car swishes by too close and covers me in muddy water. I nod in appreciation. I never did understand the self-righteous outrage at the New Yorkers who didn't do anything about Kitty Genovese being killed in front of them. We all allow evil to happen. It's a fact of life. The Germans can't be blamed, nor can I, sitting here in the dirt while the war is going on in Vietnam.

"Are you lost?" says a woman's voice: the last of the Just speaking.

I stand up, trying to look less ridiculous, and answer the nondescript face under the umbrella.

"I'm looking for a hospital."

"You're quite near one. Straight up two blocks and turn left. You'd better hurry and get out of the wet."

I move automatically in the direction I've been pointed. I guess I've decided on a solution. Wherever they'll send me will be okay, either the mental ward or ear, nose and throat. It doesn't matter. I can't stop shivering. Each step of the uphill walk sends pain waves through my body. I find the hospital: an old building, gray and deserted in the rain, uninviting. Dragging myself up the wide stairs to the reception desk, as the walls again begin to disintegrate, I decide to ask for psychiatry.

The receptionist pauses in her gum-cracking. "Just follow

the yellow brick road, honey," and she returns to her magazine.

I try to find meaning in her answer; maybe it's a test. Steam rises from my wet clothes in the warmth of the heated building.

"Is that a joke?"

She looks up, startled to see me still standing there.

"Of course not, honey. Look on the floor where you're standing. See all the colored lines? You follow the yellow one. Takes you right to psychiatric."

I giggle. "Toto, Toto," I call, but she doesn't laugh.

A straightened rainbow leads down the hall. I start off, wary of witches. It's a many-colored coat given to me by my father. The threads unravel right and left until I am left alone with yellow, looking for the Emerald City. I find a nurse in a glass booth.

"Are you accused of some heinous crime?" I ask her.

"Name, please," she says, not appreciating the joke.

"It doesn't matter."

"But of course it does. You won't see anyone without giving your name."

"But I have nowhere to go."

I start to cry.

"Wait here."

She exits out the back of the glass booth. What am I doing here? I should be home filling out university applications. The big, opaque glass doors at the end of the hall open and a tall woman in a white coat nods for me to come in.

She leads me to a small cubicle and closes the door, seating us on either side of a large desk, a yellow pad of paper marking the boundary. Her face is craggy as a mountain side and her voice is gruff.

169

"Now right off, I need to know what kind of drugs you're on."

"But I'm not on any."

"We'll give you a blood test, you know."

I don't respond.

"Why wouldn't you give the receptionist your name?"

Her voice now has a hint of kindness in it, and I wish I could curl up in her lap.

"I don't have a name anymore. It was taken from me. I really am nobody at all."

I beg her with my eyes to hug me.

"I understand what you mean. But you also have a name and address. So tell me them, please."

I want to tell her, but my throat feels glued shut and I can't remember my address. I say my old name.

"Do you live in San Francisco?"

I nod no.

"Are you a runaway?"

I nod yes.

She finds that significant, and pauses, pencil to cheek. I have a title now, but it's a lie. Really, I'm not a runaway but a goody-goody who let her parents know where she was, got a job and supported herself. I'm not on drugs and I'm not a raving lunatic. I'm so boring, I'm putting myself to sleep. Her next question doesn't surprise me.

"Why are you here?"

"I really don't know where else to be. I don't belong anywhere."

She scribbles on the yellow pad.

"But why a psychiatric ward? Why not a city-sponsored hostel?"

"Two reasons: I feel I'm going insane, and I want to die."

She nods and continues to scribble. The woman has understood me. Her intelligent eyes, emphasized by her

170

heavy-framed glasses, have grasped the emptiness behind my words and she is ready to offer me a haven. I sit quietly at ease, safe at last.

"Okay, my dear, we'll keep you with us for a while."

She turns the yellow pad in my direction, handing me the pen.

"And now if you'll just sign here."

At the sound of the familiar words, a shiver runs down my spine. I try to write, but the ink won't come out of the pen.

"What's the matter, dear?" She's already standing.

"I . . . uh . . . what is . . . "

"What is what, dear?" Her voice is less kind.

My tongue feels full of Novocaine and I pronounce each word with difficulty.

"What am I signing?"

The psychiatrist sits back in her chair, annoyed at my question.

"It's a request to enter the hospital: voluntary commitment we call it. You ask to be admitted for an observatory period of seventeen days. Now come on, my dear, and we'll find you some dry clothes."

The pen still refuses to write.

"Seventeen days," I repeat.

I try to get the doctor to look at me, but her eyes, though aimed in my direction, aren't seeing.

"Well?"

"What if I want to leave sooner?"

Her eyes narrow. There's a glint of cunning in them that I didn't see before.

"You are signing a self-commitment. You place yourself in our hands, become our responsibility. You will stay for the time required to evaluate your situation and receive whatever treatment is needed to stabilize your condition."

She pauses, her eyes boring into mine, testing for a

reaction. I feel my will being sapped from me, but my hand still will not write. My voice speaks of its own accord, tongue fuzzy and thick with the effort.

"What kind of treatment?"

She stares at me and then slowly smiles, almost in triumph. Her hand reaches out and takes the pen from mine, the yellow pad is turned back in her direction.

"I think, dear, you better find another place to crash for the night."

I don't move.

"You don't seem to understand. You are not being admitted to this hospital. I have to get back to the ward now, and I would appreciate your leaving my office." She stands.

"No." I start to cry.

Her voice toughens. "We don't have time for these kind of games here. This is a place for people who really need help, not a five-star hotel catering to a spoiled child's tantrums. I am asking you politely, for the last time, to leave, or I will have to call for more unpleasant means to get rid of you."

"Why? At least tell me what I did wrong. I'm sorry I asked questions. I knew it was wrong, but I couldn't stop myself. Please, I need you to help me."

Giant sobs surge out of my body. She pushes a piece of paper into my hand.

"I've written you a prescription for some Valium. That should alleviate the hysterics. Now will you please leave."

I shake my head miserably. I'm beyond all caring. My body will no longer function to my brain's commands. I couldn't get up if I wanted to.

"Well, I'm very sorry, but this behavior just won't do." She reaches for the telephone. "I'll need some assistance here."

Within seconds the door swings open and two big men in white clothes appear. They move gently towards me.

172

"Come on, sister. It's time to go."

A surge of energy pulses through me and I jump up from the chair and run out of the room, leaving their surprised cries behind me. I sprint down the corridor until my eye catches a small door to the right. I reach out my hand, fling it open and throw myself into the smell of ammonia and the feel of brush and rag, closing the door behind me. Outside I can hear the sound of feet running; inside are my pounding heart and gasping breath. I clutch a long wooden handle to me, ready to defend myself, and wait for the door to be opened. Surely they will give me a shot and put me to bed.

The door opens and one of the men grabs me roughly and pulls me out.

"Enough fun and games, honey. The doc says you're going home."

"No!"

I scream, surprising myself at the volume. I start to kick and bite, with the curious sensation that at the same time I am somewhere else, filming the scene from above. I look down at the two men dragging me, twisting and crying, through the glass doors and down the yellow line. The receptionist rises to watch as they pull my non-resisting body out the main door, my feet bumping down the steps, and deposit me under a tree on the front lawn, my prescription clutched in my hand. The grass is wet from the rain.

"That's as far as this taxi goes, girl. Now you go home and get some sleep."

Hands clasped around legs and head pressed into knees, I will myself into microscopic dotness and onward into nothing, the pain in my throat disappearing along the way. I am not. Nothing from inside and nothing from without. There is no sound, no smell, no touch. There is no thought process, no recording mechanism, no consciousness. I am invisible. I am dead and I have avoided the ugliness of fingers gouging holes in ceiling, scrambles for the last gasp of air. The threat of Zyklon-B is over. I am at peace.

A long time passes and the wet seeps through my jeans. My thighs are chafed and hurting, and death recedes as a viable option. In fact, the whole episode begins to seem extremely embarrassing and pretentious. Who do I think I am to rate psychiatric treatment? You have to exist before you can be treated. There has to be someone in there to treat. Even suicide is an action done by the living, a thing human in its freedom of choice. We hollow shells, however, just move around and function until somebody else pulls the plug. Non cognito ergo non sum. I go home.

CHAPTER 20

"That doctor was a cunt. But she also did you a big favor, kicking you out. Those places can wreck a person," says Ernie over the phone, his voice light, but caring. "Now if it's a diagnosis you want, I will be happy to give it to you. You have insufficient personality. Don't laugh. That's a real psychiatric category, and I should know. Some of my best friends have insufficient personalities, and I'm always there for them, the one to supply what's missing."

"I describe to you the near end of my life and you make it sound like a vitamin deficiency. A little one-a-day brand and I'll be okay. Ernie, you're not taking me seriously."

There's a pause where I hear his soft breathing.

"That's where you're wrong, love. I'm taking you very seriously. You see, I've been there myself, and I once lost a friend who was there too long. So I'm taking you very seriously. I'm just searching for the way to help you back."

"I'm sorry. I know what you're trying to do. But it just doesn't help. It's that nothing matters to me. Least of all myself. So, I think, why aren't I selfless and caring about others? But I'm not. I don't even care about the war. That's the worst right now. I don't care about the children being napalmed, the villages destroyed, the American guys being mutilated and killed, the monks burning themselves, the women raped, their young men wiped out. Nothing. I don't give a shit. I'm a robot, a machine, a Nazi, a . . . "

"Shut up, Snow!" His voice carries the slap he intends. "If we've finished our little self-pitying tirade to the realm of outer space, and despite the lateness of the hour, I will come over there."

His anger frightens me, but I tell him to come. Maybe he'll slap me around a little. Maybe that's what I need. Perhaps I'll even get a fatal injury and end my life in a picturesque slaying. Nothing seems real. Nothing is mine. The apartment is sterile and unclaimed. I ransack my drawers, looking for some clue, some sense of identity, and find the sex magazine. And there I am. Defined. A cowardly pervert, a voyeur. I answer the door with the magazine in my hand.

"You are a very strange child," says Ernie, taking it from me. "Though I guess I sense signs of intelligence or I wouldn't be investing the amount of time that I am."

His coat is wet from the rain. He takes it off and leads me over to a cushion in the living room. We sit across from each other and I study his face, trying to read it, trying to understand how he is able to care. He lights up a joint and studies the apartment, not offering me anything to smoke and not speaking.

"What's in it for you, Ernie? You don't want sex with me. I'm not a feminist project. Do you think you're Jesus or something like that?"

His eyes laugh.

"How about I give you a massage, Snow? I bet you've never had one, have you? You don't need to do anything.

176

Just lie down on your stomach and relax. It's better if you take your clothes off, but you don't have to."

He's speaking softly and gently. I can't find any malice in him.

"Just try taking your shirt off. I won't tell."

I stretch out on the carpet and, breasts concealed, pull off my shirt.

"Nice to see you're back," he says.

I stiffen.

"Just a joke, Snow. Sorry, it wasn't funny."

Gently his fingers touch my neck, then my shoulders, then my back. Sensing, probing, they ask my body questions. Where does it hurt? What's wrong in there? And slowly I relax, wiping out all sense of anything except his touch, and I let my body answer him.

"Thatta girl."

His fingers begin to knead harder, moving down my back, pausing sometimes to concentrate on some inner discord that I send him. I begin to feel like an ice field melting.

"I'm going to take off your jeans. And your underpants. Just lie still and trust me."

He slips off my clothes, like a parent undressing a sleepy child, and I'm not afraid. Now his hands are free to slide down my spine and onto the muscles of buttocks, thighs and calves. He plays the entire length of my being and what has always been a patchwork of appendages: either too long or too short, too thin or too fat, parts needing fixing, to be sucked in or filled out, hidden or "enhanced." All the parts now become a unity. Never have I felt my body of one piece before, one long, flowing structure. I sigh. Ernie chuckles, continuing to pour his warm energy into me, until all the ice is melted. Gently stroking, he warns me he will soon stop.

"Don't move for a few minutes. Just lie there and breathe."

He places a cover over me, sits down nearby, lights a joint and passes it.

I am rid of an ache that's been there so long I forgot I had it. It's disappeared and I'm left suddenly lighter; breathing freely, noticing colors and tastes with a new intensity. I feel the soft nap of the rug, the weight of the blanket, the dope sliding through my head and my body singing. I realize how silent it used to be in there. Opening my eyes I see Ernie gazing off into some private worlds of his own.

"Thanks."

He looks me in the eyes and there is a newness there between us.

"Think nothing of it, chicken. Now get up and fix us some coffee and we'll talk."

I wrap the blanket around me and fix the coffee. The kitchen is no longer sterile but full of brightly colored things, each with its use and purpose.

"Will you marry me?" I ask him.

"Not a good idea. We'd cramp each other's style. Besides, you're too weird for me. Like this business about not caring about the burning monks. What's that all about?"

I sip my coffee.

"It's actually very simple. I feel good now, but I usually don't feel anything. Other people are dying and I don't feel for them either. I have no social conscience, therefore no right to be in this world."

"The old death sentence, huh?"

"Yeah. You got it."

"That's really silly, Snow."

He catches me off guard. I start to laugh and he joins in. I laugh so hard that the coffee comes out my nose, and that sends Ernie into hysterics. Tears stream down our faces and we clutch our sides, trying to stop as each one's sputters sends the other off again.

"Good weed," he says. "Hey, Snow, are you really into that fuck and suck in black leather stuff? I wouldn't have guessed it. But then you're full of surprises."

"No. I'm not."

"Too bad."

"What?"

"You could make a mint out here. You look so virginal, and if you could learn to live with the camera, you could have yourself an adoring public. Movies, Snow, as in porno and blue. Now don't go catatonic on me. You were carrying that magazine around, weren't you? It's just a thought. You don't want to be in show biz, you don't have to."

"It's not that, Ernie. I was just wondering what my mother would say."

"Honey, I'm just making conversation."

"But maybe it's not a bad idea. I couldn't do any more damage to my image than I've already done. I'm already not fit for suburban consumption. I've only filed one university application. I gave up a good job as counselor at my old sleep-away camp. It's really just a small jump from there to making a living with somebody's penis in my mouth. I'm going to seriously consider it."

"You're feeling better, aren't you?"

"I am. But what about Vietnam?"

"No, that's the wrong setting for porno. Not now anyway, it's too controversial. Maybe in another twenty years or so, in retrospect."

I can't help myself, he makes me smile again.

"You won't deal with my profound moral crisis, will you? So I'll ask it this way: how come you're not in Vietnam?"

"That's easy. I went to my induction physical in my lacy

pink underpants. And, to be extra sure, I gained weight until my blood sugar was so high I couldn't miss."

"So you don't believe in the war."

"It's been my experience that those who are heavily involved with *believing* and *not believing*," he drawls out the word, "are having a rather dry sexual period. If they would only turn to me for help, I'm sure I could alleviate most political unrest in the world today."

"What about the war?"

"I hate the war."

"So, Ernie, that's exactly my point. You and I hate the war and we do nothing about it. We're no different from the Germans who said they didn't know what was happening. We are the Nazis."

"No. That's not right, Snow. Thanks to TV, you and I know exactly what's happening. And I had no second thoughts about wearing my pink underpants to induction, as I don't when I recommend the procedure to all my friends. Lovey, don't call me a Nazi. Your middle-class guilt tripping is not going to work on me. I'm no longer the little kid who wrapped up his lunch sandwich and stuffed it in the mailbox to be delivered to the starving children in China. Cute, but ridiculous. I'm too old and I've seen too much to indulge in dramatic gestures. Now I just concentrate on staying warm and dry."

"I've hurt you, haven't I? You come to pull me out of a slough of despond and I call you a Nazi. Strange way to show gratitude, huh? Do you want to see my magazine?"

"It's okay, kid. I get edgy too about the anti-war topic, but that's my own stuff. You see, my lover is a liberal and constantly inviting me to show up at sit-ins and jump-ins and cry-ins. The only trouble is that when we're there together I'm not supposed to go near him. He's a chicken shit. His wife deserves him. You are better, aren't you, Snow?"

"Much better. You really are nice to me, Ernie. I don't know how to thank you either. I'd like to go to bed with you but you're a foreign country that doesn't take that kind of currency. Do you know what I mean?"

"Yeah, I know. You don't need to pay me back. I told you once, you're my friend, and I help my friends. Period. Now, I'm going to teach you to play backgammon. It's part of the therapeutic procedure."

He takes a wooden box out of his jacket.

I've never been good at games. I always lose, and if I'm on a team, the whole team loses. I don't have good game karma. No matter on what board of life I'm playing, I'll lose: Clue, War, Snakes and Ladders, it doesn't matter. My brother always enjoyed playing with me. Ernie probably won't.

The round pieces feel like smooth pebbles. I mirror match Ernie, setting them on the board, and listen as he explains the game carefully and patiently until he forces my mind to start up again.

"For the first game I'll tell you what I think is the best move for each combination you roll with your dice, then you're on your own."

We play our practice game, he smiles and I learn. The second game Ernie concentrates on his own moves, grunting occasionally to indicate approval of mine. I concentrate only on the dice and game pieces, moving step by step according to what I've learned. I win the game.

"So, my little chickadee, you've beaten the wizard. And the exhausted wizard has used up his bag of tricks for the evening." He cups my chin in his hand. "You gonna be okay?"

"Yeah."

I look him in the eyes and he seems satisfied.

"What would have been, Ernie, if you weren't there to help me?"

"You would have found a way out, sweetie. You're a survivor. And you can be proud that you are. I'm one too, and I know how hard it is to leave the others drowning in the mud. But you need to know that a lot of them are just waiting there under the bridge to drag you down with them. So stay on the dry ground, munchkin, and watch out for the trolls."

He kisses me on the forehead and leaves.

It's almost dawn. I'm alive, a survivor. The thought rolls like a ship without an anchor inside me. A survivor is someone who struggles and lives to tell about it. Bad things happen, he overcomes them, and therefore he has a right to be. But I, on the other hand, have not struggled, have had no outside obstacles to wage war against. Does inner struggle count? Ernie says it does. And, if so, do I honestly struggle on that front or am I something that is tipped over to say "Mama" or flipped on to run around a track? Life would be easier if I'd been placed in a concentration camp. Then I could have been lifted out of banality and lived or died with a purpose. Even the subjects of those experiments – good lab animals letting posterity know at what temperatures the human freezes, or how much pain one twin will inflict on another – died for a reason.

Morning comes and the phone rings.

"Hello, Snow. This is Langley."

My heart stops.

"I'm sorry I didn't catch you all week. Just want to make sure that our weekend is still on."

"Grghhhh."

"Snow, are you okay?"

"Fine. I'm fine."

"You're not really up yet, are you? I'm sorry, I wanted to catch you before you left for work."

"Langley, I'm glad you called. I have a cold, that's all. And, to tell you the truth, I'm a little surprised. I sort of felt you'd changed your mind about the weekend."

"Why would you think that?"

To this I have no answer.

"I've got everything arranged to get away. The cottage is ready, I've bought some good wine and a little dope. I can get some mescaline too, if you'd like."

"Yeah, sure."

"Get your stuff ready now. I'll pick you up right after work. I'm looking forward to this weekend, Snow, and especially to making love with you."

"And I feel like an alchemist who's just discovered ether."

"And that's why I like you so much. Because you say things like that. Now take it easy today and get rid of that cold. You are to be perfectly healthy by this afternoon. In fact, take the day off work. I'll see that the boss doesn't fire you."

It's still raining outside as I crawl into bed. I wonder how Valium mixes with mescaline. I wonder if I need to rethink my philosophy of life. I wonder at the length of one night.

CHAPTER 21

*T*he sun is shining and the yellow and red juices from the dead bugs drip down the windshield. I listen to their soft splat as they are battered by the wind against the car. Langley and I, enclosed inside this insect graveyard, speed towards Mendocino; cooled air comforting us, John Denver music playing background to the squish of the bugs.

We haven't said more than two words since he picked me up and carried my overnight case to the car. Nor have we touched. Wearing the long white Mexican dress I bought with Ernie was a mistake. I must look like a virgin sacrifice instead of a woman off for a fun time. Langley, in jeans and T-shirt, has lightened his Max Von Sydow image and is looking young, healthy and relaxed. I'm afraid to speak, afraid of pushing him away, of further destroying whatever fantasy he's living in.

Once again I glide through redwoods and up a dirt road. This time the car stops in front of a wooden cabin.

"We're here."

He opens the door to let me out into a waft of sticky, hot

air. I shield my eyes and look around. The cabin, sheltered by trees, is totally isolated.

"My friend who owns this place values his privacy."

He fits the key in the door.

"I'm feeling shy too, Snow. We need to get used to each other."

In a gallant sweeping gesture he opens the door, motioning for me to enter.

The shades are drawn and my eyes adjust slowly to the darkness. Langley crosses and opens a window and the first thing I see is the large bed. Frozen by the door I make my eyes move on to take in the rest of the space: the giant braid rug covering the central floor area, the book-lined walls, the kitchen separated by a low bar partition. Langley checks in the fridge, then leans across the bar and smiles.

"What I suggest is that we go for a swim. It will give us an activity and get our minds off the tension. There's a path behind the cabin to the river, to a sandy beach of our own. There's the bathroom. Go change into your bathing suit."

I smile gratefully. The bathroom is huge, with a sunken tub, a sauna room and two entire walls mirrored from floor to ceiling. I watch the girl as she pulls off her white dress, and her movements please me, graceful and sure. Then, for the first time, I see her naked, and gasp, shocked. She is very pretty, her body young and firm and well-proportioned. I can see her from behind in the opposite mirror, her hair curled on her back like in a painting. Why didn't anyone ever tell her?

I take out my bikini, white with tiny blue polka dots, and put it on. This picture I've seen before in photos, and all the old criticisms return. Quickly I toss on a T-shirt and go out.

"Ready?"

He's wearing a black bathing suit and white sweatshirt, his

185

long tanned legs are in sandals. He grabs a blanket, hands me a thermos and heads out the door.

The screen door bangs behind us and I follow him through the trees to the bank of a quiet pool created by the river. There is a patch of sand not much bigger than the blanket, warm from the day's sunshine.

"You like?"

"It's lovely. Does your friend own the land too?"

"Yes."

Langley pulls off his shirt. His chest is smooth, with a few soft whorls of hair. He takes a pipe and a small packet from the shirt. I focus straight ahead, suck in my stomach and pull off the T-shirt, then close my eyes and stretch out on my back, bending one leg at the knee to prevent thigh spread.

I let the sun embrace, warm and fondle me, pretending that Langley isn't there. The sun is my one true love, constant and gentle, asking nothing, spilling itself into my pores. It fills and nourishes me, makes me pregnant with its sun child, a radiant ball of fire and joy and laughter.

A shadow cools my face, and I open my eyes to see Langley looking down at me, his eyes searching mine and finding there a happy nakedness that I haven't time to hide.

"You're very beautiful, Snow."

I almost believe him.

"Let's have a puff or two together."

He lights the tiny-bowled pipe and inhales, making the small dark cake inside glow. A sweet smell curls me towards him. I inhale, burn my throat, and on my next turn take it slower until my head begins to vibrate and fill with jungles: wild animals slinking through the trees, ready to pounce and rip their prey. I can't open my eyes to ward them off and, shivering, reach for Langley, not sure if I'll find him. But he pulls me in and enfolds me, his arms clasped behind my back, pressing me against his chest as if to strain me through his skin.

"Shhhh, my love. Don't be frightened."

The wild animals howl outside our cave and I cling to him for protection. He rocks me in his arms with endless patience, muttering soothing noises to ease my terror. Slowly the fire warms me and I begin to believe it will keep the wild things at bay. I can loosen my grasp and breathe normally. Langley feels the tension leave and softly strokes my neck and back as I lay cuddled on him, his fingers sending electric messages through my skin. Our breathing is now in sync, like thunder, waiting. I watch from above as his fingers trace my back, each time jumping the barrier of the bikini string, and I will him to interrupt the rhythm and pull the string open and leave my back uncluttered to his touch. I feel my breasts swell beneath me, begging for his hands to find them, but Langley just continues to caress until I can't bear it anymore. I pull myself up to face him and reach my arm around to pull the tie.

He watches quietly as I remove the top, and when my breasts spill free, he sucks in his breath, a quick gasp, and then smiles. But he still doesn't touch. Of their own accord my nipples reach towards him, and I'm embarrassed and confused.

"Don't you want me, Langley?"

He laughs. "Just look between my legs and you'll have your answer. Are you sure you want me? I want to be sure, to hear you say it."

"I want you, Langley. Please."

He thanks me with his eyes and releases whatever barrier was holding him, showing me the hunger and wanting underneath.

"Come nearer to me."

Now he is fighting between control and something more

savage. He reaches out and cups my breasts. I push forward into his hands.

"Jesus, Snow. You're going to have to lie down now. I can't wait, honey."

He gently slides the bikini bottoms down my legs. Again there is the soft gasp, almost of wonder, and then he stands beside me, pulling off his trunks. His penis seems huge, straight out in front of him.

He kneels beside me on the blanket and touches with his fingers inside.

"Oh, my sweet baby. Thank you. You're wet. I was so afraid I'd hurt you."

His fingers open me and he guides himself in.

"Oh Jesus, sweet Jesus."

Propped on his arms, his eyes glazed, he trembles and begins to thrust hard, out of control. My hips move to counterbalance, my knees bend to angle myself towards him. He moves like an animal above me, his moaning growing in intensity, eyes now open, now closed, faster and faster, until open-mouthed he screams, pulses inside and collapses, slick-skinned and panting, with all his weight on top of me. I hold him, feeling like a tender mother, kiss his ear and stroke his head while his body settles.

"I'm sorry, Snow. I didn't plan for it to be like that. The way you said you want me, and then your breasts filling my hands, I couldn't help myself. The old impulse system just took over. I'll make it up to you, though. I promise."

I try to look wise and forgiving.

"Come on, precious one. Let's swim, get dressed and I'll take you into town for dinner."

The tension gone, we swim naked in the pool, playing and splashing. I feel safe and warm now with Langley; sex finished, over the edge of will we or won't we, over the fear that he'll roll off, mission accomplished, viewing me as a dirty disposable receptacle for his chemical waste products. He's passed his test; still kind and caring, recognizing the intimacy we've shared, continuing to look at my body as pleasing to him.

The small restaurant is candle-lit. Two other couples whisper to each other, and Bob Dylan's strange voice serenades from the stereo.

"Hello, Langley. Good to see you again. And your charming companion."

"Snow, this is Burt, the owner. Burt, Snow."

I try not to wonder how many times Langley was here before. He's totally attentive, orders steak, baked potatoes, salad, red wine. He reaches out to touch me.

"Just making sure it's all real."

"Is it?"

"As real as steak and potatoes."

It's so easy to be happy, turn off the doubting, nagging voice and smile.

Back at the cabin Langley lights a fire and on the braided rug explains to me, with slow and exquisite control of fingers, mouth and penis, what he felt he'd denied me before. In bed he cradles me in his arms and I fall asleep, hearing him whisper "darling, darling" in my ear.

In the morning he brings coffee.

"I've been watching you sleep. You were dreaming, weren't you? What about?"

"You don't want to know."

"Why?"

"It's depressing."

"Try me."

"All right. I was dreaming about your wife and kids. I was wondering where's the lie. To them or to me."

"There's no lie, Snow. My wife is my best friend, my

companion in life. She understands my need for private space, for private friends. I love my family very much, Snow. And I love you."

"Where do they think you are this weekend?"

"At the cabin. Here. They don't know I'm with you of course. There's no need to cause needless suffering, is there?"

"No, of course not."

"Now, would you like to lie around and be depressed, considering questions of morality and guilt, or get up and have some breakfast? And, furthermore, if you're a good girl and stop frowning, I have a little surprise for you."

The surprise is the small mescaline pill we take with our orange juice, a pill that dispels all further doubts and dilemmas.

It begins on our beach with a change in the texture of the wind. The air becomes a multitude of different temperatured currents instead of a solid mass. The sky prisms into colored angles, arches and caves. Langley's face is a kaleidoscope; only his eyes, two warm lamps, stay stable. At some point we swim and the water flows right through us. He laughs as he sees my astonishment.

"The molecules change. You'll get used to it."

The rest of the day passes, examining fingers, toes and tree bark.

In the evening Langley brings back Chinese food in white cardboard containers. We sit on the rug in front of the fire, feeding each other with fingers and drinking wine from a bottle. I stroke him: beginning with his face, with the most delicate of movements, and move down his body until my hand dips inside his trousers and fondles, and he needs to unzip to give himself more room.

"You have a green thumb, you know. You make things grow."

I wake on Sunday to find him staring wide-eyed at the ceiling.

"You've been up long?"

"A while."

He turns and his eyes are full of tears.

"I don't want this to be over, do you? I want to go away with you right now to some island where we'll live in a little hut, never wear clothes, catch shrimp, write poetry and paint."

He grabs me to him and holds me so tightly I can hardly breathe. I pull away gently.

"Don't feel so sad, Langley. We have plenty of time ahead of us, don't we? I'm here and I love you."

"You mean that, don't you?"

"Yes."

He relaxes, closes his eyes and sleeps again, leaving me to stare at the ceiling.

Later, our things gathered in the car and the cabin closed, I almost ask how many other women have been here with him. I almost ask what he means by love. He drives me home.

"Snow, I hate good-byes. So I'll just say thanks for the beautiful time we had together."

He hands me my bag.

"I'll see you tomorrow, Langley. It was wonderful."

He doesn't turn but waves his hand in a little movement and drives away. There's a dead cat on the sidewalk.

CHAPTER 22

"*A*nd when I got to work this morning he wasn't there. That's the end of the story."

"Have another cookie."

She pushes the oatmeal chocolate chip cookies nearer and I take one. Her name is Margie and she's in her thirties, hair pulled back in a blond ponytail. Though large-boned, no makeup and clothed in a man's shirt and jeans, she carries her body with dignity, like a dancer. Within minutes of entering her house I knew her children were of high school age and too old for GROWTH's program. I needed to have moved on, but instead asked to use her bathroom and then stayed for a cup of coffee and started to talk and pile moist Kleenex by my mug.

"Afterwards I asked my car boss where he was, and she said that he'd gone abroad to a seminar he's giving in Germany on management techniques. It was all planned, you see. Not an emergency that came up or something. He knew he'd be going away all the time he was with me and never said anything."

Margie nods.

"My car boss, Bridget, looked at me funny too, like she

192

knew where I'd been all weekend, and, you know, like she's heard the story before."

I start to cry again and Margie hands me another Kleenex.

"I'm sorry for wasting your time. I feel like such a yoyo and I can't help myself. When he wanted me I felt wonderful, now he doesn't and I'm suicidal. I'm sorry. I'm probably lousing up your whole schedule here."

"Well, it's not exactly how I planned to spend my morning, but it's not an unwelcome diversion. I've always been suspicious of this door-to-door stuff, and you've given me a behind-the-scenes look that helps confirm my suspicions."

"Terrific."

"When's he supposed to be back?"

"In a week. But I'll have to quit before then. It's too humiliating. I couldn't bear for him to ignore me. Or to watch him inviting some other new recruit to counseling sessions in his office."

Margie stands and moves out of sight to her service porch.

"The clothes have finished their spin cycle. I've got to get them into the dryer. Hang on, I'll be right back."

"I should go. You're busy."

I take another cookie. On the bright yellow kitchen wall is a poster of an aproned woman, baby on one arm, broom in the other. In her teeth she clenches a book, *Modern Existentialism*. The poster is captioned "The Liberated Woman." Margie finds me studying it.

"My husband gave me that for Mother's Day. It's supposed to be a joke."

"Oh dear."

"What? You've got something against Mother's Day?"

"No."

I'm embarrassed to look at her and stare at the cookie crumbs on the table.

"I forgot you were a wife and mother, that's all. All this time I've been telling you about my miseries and I forgot who you are."

She laughs and pours more coffee.

"Though on some levels banal, your miserable story does have universal elements that are touching, even to a wife and mother. And if we are to continue this conversation, I must insist that you accept the fact that persons like me, of this category, are at moments, anyway, also human."

I smile and she gives my head a pat.

"Now, as far as the wife in your story goes, I don't particularly identify with her. In fact, if what your boss says about her is true, then she gets what she deserves. All that understanding between them sounds like a pile of manure to me. It's more like she has no pride or self-respect. But I won't go into that. Now, if you want to hear what I've got to say about you, just say so."

"Of course I do. I need help making sense out of all this."

"Okay. The way I see it, your Langley is used to, and counting on, just the kind of victimized thinking you're doing. That is, by the time he returns, out of embarrassment and whatever, you'll have folded your tents and disappeared, leaving no untidy messes behind for him to clean up. What I suggest you do is stick around, not be a victim, and give him and yourself a surprise. See what happens."

I take another cookie.

"Just like you said, you're supposed to fade out now and be a beautiful memory for him, another successful conquest. He's guilt-free, never seeing your hurt or your anger, and comforting himself with the thought that he gave you a few days you'll never forget. He actually believes that you'll never get that kind of loving again, that he's given you this great gift."

"Hasn't he?"

"Oh, my poor angel."

She looks at her watch and makes a decision.

"Listen, I've got an hour before I pick up my youngest from school and get her over to her ballet lesson. So if you're willing to listen quietly, I'll take the time and tell you a story about me and a friend of mine, a woman friend, and how I learned what giving really is. The kind where it goes on and on and where you don't skulk away from it. You want to hear?"

"I'm not sure I really do."

"I used to have this friend called Annie. She was only a year younger than me but she made it seem like more, always asking for advice and telling me about her miseries. Take note, by the way, that this was before I was married and had kids. Even then I put out maternal, come-ask-me-about-life-on-earth vibes. Anyway, I was flattered by her attitude, but it also made me feel responsible. She trusted me so much and even then I knew trust isn't something you take lightly. You don't play around with it for a weekend. God, all of a sudden I feel so old telling you all this. Maybe your friend has it figured out right after all. Live for the moment and everything."

"Hey, Margie, please go on. You're saying things that are important."

"Okay, I'll skip to the day it started getting heavy. We were at this Mexican place for lunch. Annie always ate so slowly it drove me up a wall. I was finished and she was still pecking at some minuscule particle, talking about some fight with her boyfriend who didn't understand her. I did my best to control my irritation and act motherly. She looked so vulnerable and open and, of course, getting a lot of knocks for looking that way. I thought I could protect her, teach her to toughen up a little, not be so, 'Why can't everybody just love each other?' In other words, give her a little gift so she wouldn't hurt so bad, finish lunch and get on with my other business."

I pass Margie the cookie plate.

"Anyway, this particular day she looks up from pushing the crumbs around and tells me she's got a mole on her leg that's all of a sudden started getting bigger. She's scared to get it checked at the doctor's. You sure you want me to go on?"

I contemplate getting up and trying to squeeze in an encyclopedia sale before I've got to meet the car.

"Yeah, Margie, go on."

"She says she got up the courage to make an appointment for the next day, but she's terrified to go herself. She won't tell her parents because they'll just fall apart. Her boyfriend's this rational creature who doesn't want to pamper to hysterics. When Annie told him about how scared she was to go get the growth checked, he told her not to make a mountain out of a molehill, and then laughed at his own joke. So there I am, knowing what I'm supposed to say and not wanting to say it. It wasn't fair. I hadn't bargained for this kind of responsibility. She was supposed to fit her troubles into my time schedule, respect my limits. However, she trusted me. And when I thought about that, I realized it was Annie who had given me the gift. So of course I told her I'd go."

"How old were you?"

"Twenty-one. And I was pretty positive that they'd tell her it was nothing. But still I felt scared of all that medical atmosphere. I'd never gone to get my breasts checked or anything and I had no idea what to expect. But it was at that moment that I made my decision to see it through. Because she trusted me. You understand? What I learned from Annie was that life throws things on you sometimes that it's not right to walk away from. You don't mess around with others'

196

trust. It diminishes your own life. You're very easy to talk to, do you know that?"

"Aren't you going to tell me the rest of the story?"

She eats a cookie.

"The next day Annie and I went to the clinic and the first big shock was that it was part of a hospital. Neither of us had been in a hospital since we were born. In the waiting room was this weary mother with a little girl who was bald, and a couple of men who seemed fairly healthy. Nobody looked at each other. Even the little girl seemed to have gotten the message not to talk about it. The nurse finally called us in, Annie getting permission for me to come with her. We got ushered into a bare office with a cute guy sitting behind a desk.

"He says, 'Tell me the story.'

"Annie blurts it out, he nods, takes a history of diseases in the family and gets up to look at the mole. I look at a painting of some sailboats placed there, I guess, to symbolize man's need to control the fates. He scribbles on some paper and without looking up says he wants to send her over to take a little test and hands me the order form. Annie sat there frozen and white. Neither of us were ready for this guy to be taking it seriously. And after about an hour when we came back to his office with another scribble, he said it short and sweet. 'You come back on Friday and we'll do some minor surgery to remove that thing for you. You'll be out the same day.'

"Annie just nodded her head, numb, and the doctor rose in his seat to indicate we were dismissed. I looked at Annie acting like a robot and stopped the scene. 'Wait a minute.'

"He sighed and sat down again, speaking before I had a chance to continue. 'It's pointless now to ask questions. We'll know nothing until after surgery. Do your friend a favor, take her out to a movie, get her mind off needless anxiety. Now, please, I have patients with real problems to take care of.' "

"I know the rest of the story. She had a 'real' problem, right?"

"Annie asked me to come and see her after surgery. By now I felt honored when she turned to me, let in on a whole mysterious world through her invitation. She was whoozy, smiled and nodded off into some other reality. I sat by her for a while and then a nurse collared me and led me into a closed room with the young doctor. 'Where are her parents?'

"I explained that Annie didn't want to frighten her mom and dad or deal with having to take care of them, so she hadn't told them anything about this.

" 'Well, as you seem to be the closest one to her, I'll tell you what we've found.' He still wouldn't look at me. 'She has cancer. Malignant melanoma, to be precise, which means she has a very poor prognosis.'

" 'Does that mean she's going to die?'

" 'Yes. Most likely within three months to a year.'

"He looked up for a split second, then caught my eye and immediately regretted it.

" 'There are treatment programs and further surgery that can make the chances more likely that it will be the year rather than the three months. This, of course, will be decided by the physician in charge of follow-up in conjunction with the patient.'

" 'Who tells her?'

" 'You can. I can.'

"This time he actually looked straight at me and held it. It was like he was testing my right to criticize him. So I said I would tell her."

"Margie, I'm having a hard time listening to this. I feel so worm-like and self-pitying next to you. Like now all I can think about is whether I've got some mole that might be growing. Where did you get the courage?"

Margie grabs me by the chin and holds my head rooted in front of her.

"You're missing the point. Don't think I wasn't checking out freckles every night too. So what?! All Annie and I did was keep it human, that's all."

She lets go of my chin.

"I told Annie. It wasn't that hard. She whimpered at first, like a dog who's been whipped, then she laid her head in my lap and sobbed and I stroked her and we talked. I didn't hurt your chin, did I?"

"No."

"After that, she didn't seem to need me that much. She got her life organized in between treatments, traveling, taking courses, meeting people. When we were together it was terrific, different from anything I'd ever known. I found myself savoring little details of a porch or a shirt or a conversation, tasting every chocolate chip in my ice cream. It was so intense that I was glad I had time intervals in between to catch up with myself. I learned a lot about how to value life."

Margie pauses for some inside time, then back to me.

"I don't mean to make the whole thing sound like a day at Disneyland. When she had to go to the hospital to get part of her body cut out or buy a wig for her bald head, it wasn't exactly life-is-wonderful time. And sometimes she was scared, really scared. She slept with a woolen hat on her head so nothing would zap her while she was asleep. Towards the end she was spending most of her time with her doctors in the hospital on pain medication, high and giggling. I missed her."

"Did you see her before she died?"

"Not really. Old mother Margie can't control everything."

I guess I look hurt at her reaction.

"Sorry. Guilt feelings coming through. I did talk to her. One night about two in the morning my phone rings and it's Annie calling from the hospital. She sounded just like she had a year before. She wanted my advice, and I thought for a second that maybe this cancer thing had never happened. But then she asked me this question she wouldn't have asked a year ago. What should she do with her fear of sleeping, her fear that she wouldn't wake up. Her voice was full of all that trust again. I had to tell her something. So I suggested she set her alarm clock for every half hour, then she could wake up and know she was still there. She said thank you, and died some hours later."

She looks at her watch.

"Wow – I've got to run to get my kid. Can I give you a lift?"

"No. I'm getting picked up. Margie, thanks for this morning."

She reaches out and takes my hand.

"This has been a fine morning for me too. The kind of thing I learned from Annie. And now the really last bit of sage wisdom. Don't run away from difficulties, trying to protect yourself. First of all, it usually doesn't work, they follow you around. And, secondly, you miss out on a lot of surprises, what happens after. So it hurts sometimes. You can take it. Women's pain thresholds are high and we can go deeper because of it. You shouldn't let this guy bring you down to his level. . . . "

She laughs and stops mid-sentence.

"Come on, kid, let's get out of here."

I watch her drive away in her tan station wagon and toy with the idea of never leaving her front lawn. However, this does not seem realistic. On the freeway home my car mates practise our latest GROWTH exercise: positively willing breaks in the traffic. And I think of frightened Annie and the one time when the half hour on her alarm clock rang and she didn't turn it off. The picture gives me enough push not to die or go crazy just yet, take my life a step at a time and at least see what's going on.

CHAPTER 23

And so I begin to think about life and my part in it.

Taye suggests I take her to the Universal Cafe in China-town for dinner. We sit in the back, near the smells coming from the kitchen, in a closed booth of shiny dark-brown wood with a curtain drawn across the front. Inside is a simple table, chairs, a mirror on the back wall and a button to call the waiter. It's as intimate as a car; the world is confined to our space.

Taye orders for both of us; wonton soup, mushrooms and bamboo shoots, shrimp in oyster sauce, chicken in black bean sauce and rice. The waiter is old and kind and brings us tea while we wait. The warm white porcelain cup feels good in my hands.

"So when will you be leaving?"

"And how come you're so sure that I'm leaving?"

"School starts beginning of September, right? You got that letter saying you're accepted at the university, your mother's repainting your room, and you agreed to invite me out to dinner so you could tell me you're leaving and I could have a couple of weeks to look around for someone to take your place. Aren't these enough hints?"

"But, Taye, I haven't decided yet. For all I know, maybe I'm staying the rest of my life. It's you who's always harping on my leaving. Why do you assume I'm on my way through?"

"Because you are, that's why. You're a visitor."

She sips her tea.

"I'm a visitor on earth, Taye. I don't really belong here. I'm Superman and my home planet's been destroyed. Don't laugh. I'm really serious. You may have noticed that most people have some sort of life path, they know where they've been and reach conclusions about where they're going. They talk about it, you yourself talk about it. I know what you are, what you think and a lot of the times why you think it. But, tell the truth, you can't say that about me, can you? I've lost my way, and neither you nor anybody else can find it for me. You're wrong about Toronto. I don't want to go back home, to being nice to the cleaning lady because she's working-class, to getting good grades by second guessing what another person wants to hear, to having ridiculous fights with my mother about whether my bangs are too long, and watching my father wither away inside lost dreams, to my little brother who sees me as part of the whole package, as I guess I see him."

The old waiter hooks up a warming tray to the outlet on the wall and sets down the steaming dishes. He gives us chopsticks, forks and soup spoons and ladles out our soup. Taye waits until he's gone.

"You're right. I shouldn't jump to conclusions. But you do give me the feeling I can't count on you."

I watch Taye manipulate the chopsticks, picking up minuscule grains of rice that just stick themselves to the wood. I try to imitate her, with no success, and reach for a fork.

"Snow, Snow, poor little innocent Snow. It's your first time using chopsticks, isn't it? You really should go to university or finishing school or something. Complete your education. Your mom's paid the tuition, fresh paint in your room. As for me, I have to get a roommate committed to stay for the school year. And I have to do it now before the semester starts."

"You've talked this over with your group, haven't you? They told you to get a new Snow."

"Well, certainly I discussed it. And you need to know they're all very fond of you."

"I thought you were fond of me too, goddammit. I thought Langley cared for me. What is going on here? Some kind of conspiracy?"

"Don't compare us, Snow. Men lie. They're not capable of truth with a woman. They always have some ulterior motive in mind. Eventually it won't hurt anymore, it just gets boring. You and I, on the other hand, are roommates for the summer, clear and simple. I like you, but you are really fucked up, like a lot of summer people, and now I want someone in the apartment who's more stable, more from this planet, I guess. Also, it's no good for you to try and build your life around me."

I concentrate on the shrimps in their shiny red sauce. The letter from my mother scared me, with all its plans and pronouncements: life locked into another four years. And then what? Teaching and marriage, house and kids. And after that, just summer reruns; do my jobs, fulfill their expectations.

When I was a little kid, I used to believe everybody else had their personal *TV Guide* that let them know what to expect in their lives for the coming week. Except mine never got delivered. I was embarrassed to tell anyone, so I used to creep out of bed at night and with the light from the hallway shining into my room, I would sit by the heater with the regular TV schedule, a piece of paper and a pencil in my hand, and plan out the week for myself. I would mark out my days, divided into sections of time, and for each time slot I would pencil in the name of a TV show that I would live in for those hours: *My Three Sons*, *My Friend Flicka*, *My Favorite Secretary*. This way I too had a role and life made sense. It was as good as God.

But somewhere along the line I lost my faith. I no longer believe in *TV Guide* or anything. The world is just an arbitrary set of conflicting rules, nobody's party line better than the next one's. I can no longer live in a framework.

"Good, huh?"

She devours the food in the same intense way she does everything. Nothing has more importance than the act of this minute. She's right to worry that I want to build around her, to be like her. Why shouldn't I? She has a core that shines through all the shrouds of day-to-day things, a personhood. If the Nazis killed her, they would be committing an atrocity: killing an entity, not another number.

"There's a mass demonstration against the war end of the week. You want to go? The group will be marching from downtown all the way to Golden Gate Park, hundreds of thousands. You are against the war, aren't you?"

"Of course I am. How can you even ask that?"

"I read some article about Canadians resenting the American draft resisters who've gone to Canada, taking jobs from real Canadians and like that."

"So why did you assume I was one of those? Why do you keep deciding things for me?"

Taye smiles and pushes her hair from her face.

"Have some more chicken."

She waits until I've put a piece in my mouth.

"First of all, this time I didn't assume anything. I asked

you. We've never talked about it and you might have been apathetic or something. Stop being so paranoid."

"Why did you invite me?"

She waits until I eat another bite of chicken.

"I guess I feel bad about rushing you out of the apartment, so I want to make up for it. And what you said about me and Langley being alike hurt. I want to prove you're wrong. And I think the march will be exciting for you. You've probably never been to anything like it."

"Wrong."

I finish the last of the chicken in black bean sauce.

"I was a captive participant in demonstrations from the time I was in a carriage. Everything. From Save the Canada Goose to Fluoride in the Water to Ban the Bomb."

She looks at me with a new interest.

"Sorry. But you do give the impression of knowing nothing sometimes."

"Why don't you ask questions? You don't ask me things."

"Touché."

We laugh. The waiter clears the dishes and leaves more tea and fortune cookies.

" 'Living with troubles is also a living,' " I read out loud.

" 'Marginal man has an index on life.' I think, Snow, that there is some very stoned person working in this cookie factory. But now that we're into Zen philosophizing, I'm going to ask you a question. Why do you think you're so fucked up?"

"I don't know."

"That's not fair."

"All right. I'm a product of a Marxist contradiction. They tried to grow me up on dialectical materialism in a middle-class setting and it led to disastrous psychological results. It's hard when the goal of your belief system is to plan your own withering away. But that's what I'm programmed for.

University and then self-destruction. No wonder I ran away."

Outside, the narrow streets are crowded: Chinese residents, tourists, sailors and soldiers. The stores are filled with colors: the reds, greens, golds and whites of dishes, kimonos, fans, brass, jade and ivory. Taye leads me into a kitchenware shop. There are hundreds of shelves filled with bowls of every size imaginable. Strange utensils for chopping, slicing, paring and shaping line the walls. Paper lanterns in brilliant patterns hang from the ceiling.

"I need a wok."

She looks at shallow metal pots. Outside again, she buys lichee nuts from a street vendor.

"I'd like to talk about Vietnam a little more. Ron was there before I knew him. He went mainly out of sloth, called up and no energy to get out of it. That's how he describes it. He got wounded, almost died and sent home. And then there's a cousin of mine who died in Korea. Nobody I really know. But they say he was something special. These are real issues, Snow. Not mind games in your head."

"The only people I know who were in a war are my father and his friends: glory, glory hallelujah kinds of war, good war where you go and kill the fascists. There aren't any soldiers or armies or wars in Canada now. We live with pictures of other people's disasters."

"But it could happen to you. Ron was almost killed in a war that he thought could never affect him. For your own sanity you can't be passive today, Snow. Your 'life-hasn't-shown-you-a-path' speech is something Ron might have come up with, and it's just another excuse not to make a commitment. Actually, it's also an invitation for someone else to run over you. That's the American Way."

"You're right, you know. I'll go to the demonstration."

She touches me briefly on the shoulder.

"I know that. And don't be too mad at me for my wanting to keep some distance from you. I'm too vulnerable myself and I've been burned too often. I only hold people's hands now when I know they're strong enough to hold mine back."

I see how very lonely she must be. We walk home in silence, sharing something that neither of us is willing to talk about: that we are saying good-bye without really having known each other. And I don't suppose we ever will. I'm leaving, but I don't know where I'm going. Maybe there's a People's Alternative to the C.I.A. I could be given a mission in life, defined for me by the Supreme Force. Not questioning my superiors' judgment, I could fulfill the job or be killed in the line of duty, fighting for Truth, Justice and Freedom.

"I'm not mad about you looking for another roommate, Taye. You're right to plan ahead like you do. I only wish I could see so clearly, to know what to hold on to, what to let go."

We reach the apartment and walk silently to our rooms. I don't really know why I've let this happen. When we went out this evening I had no clear intention of moving out. Or did I?

CHAPTER 24

On the podium he looks rested and shining. His eyes flicker over mine in a moment of acknowledgment. Then he passes on. I make myself look attentive, one of the gang, getting ready for my day to push my sales over the graph and into the cosmos. Franny isn't here and I take note of where her car boss is sitting to go find out what's happening.

"You are all so beautiful," sings Langley. "You are the colors of the rainbow, except more so. How wonderful it is to get back and find your perfect faces looking at me. And when I spoke in Germany I saw perfect faces there too, those faces that believe in the possibility of good and growth, those faces that exist all over the world and are willing to risk showing it. I won't pretend that being in Germany I didn't sometimes get a chill over thoughts from the history books. But I also know that evil, along with the good, seems to have been built into the universe, is part of the cycle, like death is with life, and sickness with health. I can't attempt to understand why there is evil. But I will not let it negate my ability to see the good. I will not let evil take on undue proportion. It's my choice. I can see the darkness or I can see the sun."

His voice is soaring.

"And I choose to see the sun. It's my responsibility, and I choose to see the sun. And if you seekers want to see the sun," he pauses and sweeps us into his starry eyes, "whose responsibility is it? You, Karen, whose responsibility is it?"

"Mine."

"That's right, madchen. We'll say it all together, okay? If you want to see the sun, whose job is it to make it shine?"

"Mine," we say softly, echoing.

"Now close your eyes and see the sun, really see it. See the fields and stars and the trees. No prison of mind or body can ever take that from you. No one, nothing, has the means to rob you of that choice. You are at Cause!"

I search for the sun, and it's true what he says, it's at my beck and call. I have pictures of us loving at the cabin and then stabbing flashes of hurt at abandonment. But I can choose which pictures to see. I can stay in the sun or let the shadow pull me under. I don't have to act like the prototype for weeping, hysterical, victimized woman. Just like Frodo the Hobbit, I can have a stout heart and level head if I want to. I can choose to be cool and grownup and thank Langley for what he's taught me.

"You can open your eyes, ladies. You're feeling wonderful, aren't you? And you did it all yourselves. Know that. Know that you have the power within to turn night into day. You've just done it, haven't you? 'The world is what I believe it to be.' Say it with me."

We repeat, over and over. Langley leaves the podium and walks to the back of the room, touching those near the aisle softly on the head.

When he has left the room, we rouse ourselves from the

trance and gather into our car groups. I grab Franny's car boss.

"Franny sick or something?"

"No, Snow. She's apparently gone home to her parents. She hinted at it in morning meeting last week when you weren't here."

Does she pause significantly to tell me she also knows why I was absent?

"Franny said Langley had given her new strength. We thought she meant sticking to a diet because she's been losing weight. But it seems she called Mary yesterday and informed her that she was leaving GROWTH and going home."

She passes on the information with no emotional overlay.

In the car I think about Franny and feel guilty. Franny who helped me out when I needed her. I was so caught up in my own stuff that I did nothing to reach out and find out more about her. She was someone who wanted to be my friend and I let her down. And where did I put my energy? Into Langley, who has, it seems, much greater things to do with his life than invest it in me. Franny really cared and I devalued what she gave me. I see the framed pictures in her room of her doting parents, and I'm afraid they will swallow her up into shopping baskets and cleaning bills.

We reach the drop-off corner, huddle and chant softly, "The world is what I believe it to be." I walk down the cracked sidewalk, weeds growing through, looking for my starting address. It's a poor, white neighborhood with an occasional splash of color. Harried mothers tell me they don't have time, as they drift back towards the TV, smoking cigarettes and sipping coffee. I've almost decided that today the world is not what I believe it to be, but at the eighteenth house a delicate and very young woman asks me in. Her skin is fine and freckled, her gray eyes open and trusting.

Though not much older than I am, she is the mother of a three-year-old boy. I'm sure she will buy the encyclopedias for her child.

I spread the glossy sheets over her coffee table. She answers, letter perfect, to my cues.

"Does this educational method make sense to you?"

"Certainly, yes."

"Do you understand the payment plan?"

"Yes, I do."

As I move into the home stretch, coasting downhill now, we feel good and the sun is shining on both of us. I get ready to hand her the pen, my eyes focused on the dotted line where her name will appear.

And then there is the first scream, followed by silence. We are suspended, the pen in my hand poised, about to be transferred to hers. We wait, frozen, knowing the screams will start again, and soon the high-pitched shrieks of a child move towards us.

"It's my baby."

She moves in slow motion through the swinging door into the kitchen. I follow in time to see the screen door bang open and a small body screaming "Mommy, Mommy" hurtle into the room. I can't understand his face. It seems to be entirely covered with a brown and yellow mask. And the mask is moving.

The mother stands frozen. I turn to her.

"His grandfather keeps bees."

The child's screams have turned to moans, his eyes, beginning to swell shut, are in panic.

"I'm terrified of bees," she says. "Please."

I consider leaving. Who am I to do a heroic act? But I remember my decision to take one step at a time. And this seems to be the next step.

"Just a minute, kid."

I run into the living room and grab my largest, glossy brochure, then back to the kitchen where I wave it in his face.

"This'll do it."

The boy screams louder. The bees begin to leave him and buzz in circles around the room. The mother has shrunk into a corner. I scream at her to open the door, and jumping and yelling like a maniac, I wave the bees towards it. She pulls herself together and grabbing a dish towel helps to shoo most of them out of the house.

The boy hasn't moved. He stands, whimpering and shaking, saying soft words I can't understand. Small welts are rising on his exposed face and arms. The mother approaches cautiously and bends to look in his face. I am sure that now she will finally take him in her arms and wonder whether the pain will be too much for him. She leans towards him, head lowered as if asking forgiveness, and then abruptly jerks back and moves away. The child does not even react. I feel like slapping the woman.

She turns to me, hysteria beginning to take control again.

"There's another bee. It's in his ear."

I think I'm going to throw up but move closer to the shaking boy. The bee's stinger is sticking out of his right ear, its head buried inside. It looks like it's trying to bore its way into his head, buzzing steadily, absorbed in its work. The child is hypnotized by the sound. For a moment I can't move, not out of fear but as if held back by the giant hand of Fate, my task to be only a witness. Then something else takes over and I grab the dish towel from the mother and pull the bee out, its soft insect body flapping through the terry cloth. I release him into the yard. The boy is as he has been, whimpering and alone.

"Go to your child now."

He draws away from her as if from another sting. Gently

she pulls off his shirt, and underneath are the swelling bumps.

"I think you'd better take him to a hospital. Do you want me to phone a taxi?"

"Josh, honey, we'll go to the doctor now and he'll give you some medicine to feel better."

She touches his hand and this time he melts into her.

"Well, I guess I'll be going."

She doesn't answer me, absorbed in cooing to her child.

"You should get him to a doctor soon. He might be allergic or something."

She nods.

I pack my things and leave the house, aware of the throbbing in my arms where I must have been stung. I wait on the sidewalk in front of the house until the taxi departs with mother and puffy-looking boy, releasing me from my vigil.

In pain, a wave of fatigue almost toppling me, I feel wonderful. It is the perfect outcome of Langley's lecture. I am the sun, finally a heroine; a saver of children, a courageous human being able to overcome obstacles in the cause of helping innocent humanity. The pile of baby shoes in the concentration camp has one less pair today. I have saved a child. By doing an act in time, a physical deed, I've labeled myself forever as not a Nazi. It is my first real test and I've passed. I am on the road to knighthood. Soon I will kneel and be given yet another new name. On the way home I hide my wounded arms and guard my secret from Taye, waiting to report directly to my liege lord on the morrow.

I spend the evening in my room, daubing calamine lotion on my arms and rehearsing my story for the morning meeting. I want Langley to understand and to be proud of what I've learned from him. I want him to know I value the present that he's given and that even if we're not lovers, it's okay with me and I want to be near and continue to learn from him. I want him to understand that I too can function on the cosmic level; freed from possessiveness, not trapped in petty details of who didn't call who, and angry discussions on who didn't meet what expectation. I am the heroine in my own book now. He will see the enlightenment in my eyes tomorrow and acknowledge in his own that we have touched in deep, dark places. That will be enough. My humiliation will be over and I'll know that what was between us wasn't a lie. We will be witnesses, one for the other, lending strength when doubt creeps in. What was between us was real, a meeting out of time, with no strings attached. We reached the intensity that our two energies were destined to reach, and now we move on in our separate orbits. The world is what I believe it to be. It's my first bedtime prayer since I was a child.

"You look like you've had some mystical experience," Taye says not unkindly over soft-boiled eggs in the morning.

I am charged and high, singing tunes of peace and harmony as I go into morning meeting. I catch sight of Langley talking to a new trainee and enclose them both in a beam of warmth and caring, truly wanting her experience with him to be as deep as mine was. The murmuring of the others around me is a bath of shared understanding and I wait impatiently for my turn to speak and share with them the shining rays of yesterday's experience. Never before have I felt I belonged so completely on this earth, and the experience is so new and fresh I hold my breath so as not to damage it. As Langley mounts the podium, I radiate thank you and thank you and thank you and thank you again.

"Good morning, everybody. To quote a quote from an old friend of mine, 'Today is the first day of the rest of your life.' I know we will all work together to help our new trainees who have joined us today to understand how perfectly that sentence describes us here at GROWTH. I thought I might

215

dispense with my own speech-making this morning and go right to asking for volunteers who are ready to share with us some personal experience. Yes, Jan?"

Jan tells us how she finally got up courage to phone an ex-boyfriend and tell him that she still loved him, and how it didn't hurt at all when he didn't respond. I clap loudly with the rest.

"Yes, that is unconditional love," says Langley, "and in learning to bestow it on others, we also learn to love ourselves. Thank you, Jan. And now . . ."

I feel him hesitate, not sure, then decide.

"Snow."

I tell the story of the child and the bees as I've been taught, without emotional overlay, just what happened. I don't expect reactions for this part. I wind up, though, with the realization of my heroic status and let my joy shine through, looking out at my friends and next to me to Langley, to bask in the magic of their knowing me. There is the expected pause when I finish, the tension before the applause. I smile, naked, waiting to be warmed by their response.

There is nothing. Their faces look like they are waiting for more information, and I have no idea what's missing. The trainees, picking up their cue, sit immobile. Eventually Langley's terse "Thank you, Snow" releases me to my seat. I sit there numbed, in shock, until the end of the meeting.

"You have to explain to me what went wrong."

I run after Bridget, the car boss, on our way to the car.

"What did I do? I was so proud of what happened yesterday. I didn't even tell you because I wanted to share it with the whole group today."

"It's a pity you didn't share with me first, Snow. I could have warned you. I can see you really don't understand. Your story didn't end appropriately. After mother and child were saved, you needed to use that wonderful energy you felt to go on to the next house and make a sale. Something for yourself. You were jerking off, Snow, basking in your own heroics on company time. You sounded like Don Quixote, sort of pitiful, tilting at windmills."

She smiles.

"Snow, enough of looking at the past. Now we have to get ready for the first day of the rest of our lives. You'll go out today with courage and channeled energy, find your Contact and make her the gift of buying into Choice. And, honey, if there's a disaster in your block, call a neighbor and get on with your business."

"Thanks, Bridget."

There's still so much to learn. I'm lucky they forgive so easily.

CHAPTER 25

*T*his morning Langley announces that Franny has committed suicide, jumped off the tallest building in Madison, Wisconsin. The news is sandwiched between the notification of a new addition to the sales kit and the announcement that he is leaving for Florida for a week's seminar. In the car, driving to Daly City, nobody says a word. I don't sell any encyclopedias either.

Taye spends the evening on the phone organizing for tomorrow's march against the war. I fall asleep wondering if anybody from GROWTH will be there and dream of Langley leading a contingent of Seekers in black SS uniforms. Sometime during the night the picture changes to my pushing Franny off a high building. As she falls, she looks up at me, grinning, and says, "Thanks for helping me. It's a fool-proof new method for losing weight."

As I struggle to consciousness in the morning, the boy Josh's small face, unmarked by bee stings, floats by.

Against the background of Taye's urgings to get a move on, I dress reluctantly. Who am I to march against the napalmers? Let he who is without sin cast the first stone. But

I'll go with Taye because I've promised, and it will be our last activity together. She and my mother assume I'll be leaving in a week or two. My mother has applied for me to have my own charge cards at Eaton's and Simpsons. Taye has placed a notice up at the Y.

The day is bright and clear. Taye and I pack sandwiches and thermoses with hot tea. She has prepared placards, hers in purple and gold that says "LBJ – WAR CRIMINAL," and mine in reds and oranges, "GET OUT OF VIETNAM."

"They'll be coming to get us to drive over to the starting point in a few minutes. You better take a jacket."

"Do you think any of this will make a difference, Taye?"

"If you don't think so, then why are you going?"

Because I feel like Eichmann? Because I'm worried about the banality of evil?

"I guess I don't know what else to do. I haven't got any alternative, like burning a draft card. All I can do is march. I've been sitting around watching this war on TV for too many years."

"Well, that's as good a reason as any. I don't see anything wrong with that. What's wrong with that?"

"Because if I was serious, I'd be there in Vietnam with the guerrillas."

She laughs. But it's not a joke.

The doorbell rings and Nancy is there to take us downtown. It's good to see her and Dalia, and even Gerry the militant. The traffic is so clogged we decide to walk. People are moving in from all directions, and as we move towards the clumping mass ahead, officials with armbands direct us along. Within a few moments we are swallowed by bodies, standing packed in and unable to move. I've never been in a demonstration as big as this, and I can't imagine this swelling monster getting mobilized. The five of us concentrate on staying near each other.

Nancy is worried. "I want to march with the women's groups."

Dalia pats and comforts her, and order is gradually made out of chaos. It takes about an hour to get straightened out and I relax and let myself feel the warmth of the bodies around me, using the time to estimate the amount of Naziness inside me as the loudspeakers counterpoint my train of thought.

"Free Theater Against the War, move slowly forward through the crowd. Doctors Against Death, raise your placards so we can see you. Children of Vietnam Vets, move forward. Folks, let them through."

I help a little kid forward. He's carrying a placard twice his size: "LBJ – WHY DOES MY DADDY HAVE NO LEGS?"

We move into the flank of Women against the War, thousands of women converging together: a sea of women, gathering, laughing, calling hellos. At the front of our contingent is a women's marching band dressed like Uncle Sams but with giant stuffed breasts. They're playing a medley of Dixie songs, some prancing and tossing batons. Girl children are plentiful and here and there are boys and even a sprinkling of men. But the main feeling is of female power, power born of sheer numbers. Together, as we begin to walk down the San Francisco streets, we are whole: a complete unit of tremendous energy and strength, not needing anything but ourselves. Marching with them is like the feeling I had when I first learned to ride my bike and pedaled away from my father's hand holding the bicycle seat, elated, soaring into the sky. It was only when I looked back and saw him standing forlorn and abandoned that I curbed my joy.

Taye grins at me from underneath her placard and I grin back. Some marchers have baskets of flowers to throw at passers-by on the sidewalks, and folks scramble to catch them. This is not one of the somber, slush-filled demonstrations I remember from my childhood. We are strutting, stepping high.

"I don't think it's right that I'm feeling so good," I yell at Taye.

"You're beautiful," she yells back. "We're all beautiful. And nobody is going to dare oppose this energy. Nobody around here is going to put the moves on you, and nobody is going to sell us a war. You're safe, Snow."

An older woman in front of us has heard the exchange and turns around to smile. "That's right, sister, no one can hurt you here."

I look at the men who look at us from the sidewalk, and they're not all the same. There are those, mainly the older ones, who are disgusted and angry. Among the younger guys there are some who drool and make ugly eyes. And then there are others, with open grins, who smile with their eyes too and seem not afraid of us. They look turned on to see the powerful women and I want to believe them.

"Don't believe them," says Gerry beside me.

"I suppose I shouldn't. But at least they support us against the war."

"If they are against the war or for the war, it doesn't matter. They're against us. Their whole lives are built on keeping us down. They know nothing else."

"Okay, Gerry."

"Don't patronize me," she answers.

Nancy pulls her aside into conversation. The march winds down Geary Street, which has been blocked to traffic. Policemen on tall horses escort us. I feel protected by them, while Gerry mutters "Pigs." The marching band is now playing Sousa and overhead an airplane writes the word "Peace" in giant letters in the sky. I resist asking Gerry if it matters so much if it's not a woman pilot.

It's now midmorning and the sidewalks are jammed.

Some people have brought deck chairs, others wave from high-story windows. Quite a few join in. I catch up with Taye.

"How many people are there?"

"We're expecting several hundred thousand. People came in from all over the coast. It's been very well organized. The women's groups have been on it for months."

"I can almost believe we can change things."

"Oh, Snow, of course we can. I still don't understand why you're such a cynic about political change and yet so totally naive about men."

"Got to believe in something, I guess. Why not true love, unconditional and all that?"

"You really are just a product of suburbia, aren't you? Mixed with a few flashes of old-time socialism."

"Yeah, I am. Daughter of my parents' generation of radicals: fight fascism, save your virginity and meet the next car payment. Sad but true."

"And you're letting it happen."

"What do you want, Taye? I already see the corruption at the end, so what's the point of going through the motions? I was born politically cynical. They believed in Stalin, for God's sake. I do like this march, though. I do think the United States needs to get out of southeast Asia. I'm glad to be around everybody who's saying so and I feel wonderful marching with all these women. I just don't see what it matters to some starving peasant in Vietnam."

"It would matter to me. And you'll see, Snow, we'll get out of Vietnam."

Americans are so convincing in their readiness to believe they can do anything. The march is working on me: the music, the rhythm of the walking and the pure feeling of the giant number of bodies joined in one concentrated event. After a four-hour walk we reach the park. The mass of humanity spread out in front of me is beyond my comprehension. I stop.

"Move along, Snow, we're sitting with all the women together."

Nancy pats me as she moves around the edges of our group, shepherding us through the sitting, standing, dancing, holding, laughing, drinking, smoking, eating bodies. It is the same park as when Ernie brought me here, but vibrating at a much higher frequency. We find a hill with the surrounding trees hung with signs: "Women Against the War", "Cut the Pentagon's Balls Off," etcetera.

"This must be the place," says Nancy.

I turn and watch the never-ending line of people dance into the park. Rolling Stones music pours from the loudspeakers placed in trees around us. On the far edges of the crowd are strolling policemen and white ambulances. Nancy settles me down on a blanket and hands me a joint. I smoke and the sounds and colors of the day break into fragments.

Below us, in the distance, is a wooden platform with small stick figures seated behind a table. Occasionally one stands and moves to the front of the stage, the music stops, and a voice wiggles through the sound system: "Stop the war and pain and suffering, save the children, destroy the industrialist warmongers." We applaud and yell "Right on."

Around me people are bringing out their picnics. Each group is passing to the next: drinks, smokes, cookies. Frisbee games have started over ducking heads, a couple is making love under a blanket.

"I'm sorry, I still don't understand how this is going to stop the war."

"Nancy, shut her up, will ya?" says Taye.

Nancy sighs. "Because, little Snow, nobody here will kill anybody. It's as simple as that."

223

I pause mid-bite on my salami sandwich and wave the next joint away; any more and I'll fall into a coma. Nancy has sent shivers through my body and the sun speckled through the trees is slow to warm me. Wherever I look now, I catch eyes holding mine, pouring through me with the sun. Here you are safe. Here no one will kill.

The park is singing around me. Everyone is on their feet, clapping, swaying, banging tambourines, "Let the sun shine, let the sun shine . . . " On the platform the kids from *Hair* are dancing and singing, directing the bodies in front of them. Paranoia slinks by. Is it the Fourth Reich? Now that I've finally proven my innocence, am I to be swallowed by the masses around me, the giant crowd vibrating as one, ready to be led to oppression or self-destruction, wherever an evil mind will take them?

And I know that thought is ridiculous. We're singing a song, and if any idiot should try and get up on that platform and preach a number, he'd be laughed out of the park. And what about Snow herself? No, she won't kill either. She's a little confused, but she won't kill. She's sometimes uncaring, but she's not deliberately cruel. She is condemned by this court neither to death nor life alone in Spandau. She is the one who has saved a child from bees and perhaps there is still hope for her.

I stand up and open my mouth and let the music take me. And together with the hundreds of thousands of others, sing, "Let the sun shine in."

CHAPTER 26

Dear Mom and Dad,

I'm not coming home. And, yes, this also means I'm not going to university.

I wish you guys would try and understand. I don't want you to see me as a failure, or as if I'm turning my back on all you stand for, ungrateful for all the advantages. I don't want you to spend hours examining where we went wrong. It's not a bad thing that's happening. I need to grow up, find out who I am, away from the expectations.

A friend of mine out here went home and because she believed she wasn't the "right" weight jumped off a building. I feel like I'd be killing some part of myself too if I left now, and I don't even know what part it is. I think maybe it's something that hasn't grown yet. Can you understand this? Or are you caught up in "how could she, after all we . . . "?

I'm starting to feel good. I never quite knew what that meant before. I feel like my days are beginning to be made up of small choices that are really mine, like whether to have a soft-boiled egg in the morning.

Does that sound weird? What I mean is that I'm not weighing whether I'm pleasing or antagonizing some-body, or even if the egg is good for me, but figuring out if my body really wants an egg.

I have this feeling I'm not getting through. Maybe I can explain it differently.

I went to a big anti-war demonstration. That's a good sign, right? But this time I went with my own very confused personal reasons, not like in Toronto when I went because it was the "right" thing to do. And a very strange and totally unexpected thing happened. I didn't feel self-righteous and correct, having done my bit, paid my dues. What I did feel, for the first time in my life, was hope on a global scale. There I was, with the people who are making this war, the guys who are being drafted, the ones whose families and friends voted this government in, and I was at the center of the universe. There at the park I mattered in the planetary scheme of things.

You taught me to admire those who act on princi-ples. Why do you then try and lure me home with Simpsons and Eaton's charge cards? How does it make sense for me to make big decisions based on building up a good credit rating? I want the cards, but I don't want them to decide for me. I know you see me as childish, going through a rebellious phase. If only I could take a more mature look at things, the long-range view, then I wouldn't be ruining my life. You probably think it's a pity I didn't meet some nice boy in Toronto and then none of this would ever have happened. But how do I reconcile myself to that kind of life when I know your heroes are Sacco and Van-zetti?

What would I study at university? You know, I have

226

*no idea. I always figured I would go, like kids go to
school every day. There's no choice in the matter. If
you miss a day, you bring a note from your parents. I
never in my life thought about not going. I was like a
computer, programmed by somebody else. And you
know a really scary thing? I figured out the program
stops after university. The tape just runs out. I'm not
supposed to marry, I'm not meant to have a job.
Nothing. I just finish then, eternally separated from
the working classes.*

*I hope what I'm writing makes a little sense to you.
In my fantasies you wish me well.*

Taye doesn't understand why I'm moving out.

"If you're not going home, then why are you leaving?"

"Because you were so sure I was."

"You want to punish me?"

"No, that's not it at all. You and your group, you're into
this let's-take-care-of-each-other. If I'm not totally part of
you, then I'm the potential enemy, you're suspicious of me,
always ready to cut me loose. Like the way you feel about
men. For me it's like living around one of those bug-zapping
machines. I'm the bug and I've got to be neutralized to
protect the environment."

"What is this? Another one of your SS nightmares?"

"I'd like to try and explain."

She doesn't look away.

"You decided I was going back to Canada to protect yourself, so you'd be ready for it, not to get too attached. I know
that. But it makes me feel like a dangerous bug, that you
have to defend yourself that hard so I won't hurt you. You
take care of yourself, but it leaves me feeling poisonous."

"Snow, you can stop all this garbage. You want to move
out, move out. Your rent is paid until the end of the month,

you don't owe me a thing. We will both live happily ever after. All this poison business is very weird. You might be wise to find some kind of therapy for yourself, kiddo, before you go over into completely strange territory."

"It's okay, Taye. I guess there's just no graceful way to pull away. But I do want to thank you for all the things you've tried to teach me. You and your friends just have too many strong opinions for me to handle right now. I have to come to some of my own conclusions."

The last station for good-byes and explanations is GROWTH. I phone to say I'm coming in to discuss quitting, and Mary and Langley receive me together in his office. We sit around the coffee table. I haven't been this close to him since we were at the cabin. His eyes are veiled as he lets Mary handle it.

"You said on the phone, Snow, that you wanted to discuss leaving. That means you haven't made a decision."

I can see where my answer is printed in her script. They will listen only if I say no decision has been made.

"That's right, Mary."

I can feel Langley's energy radiation change, warning lights going up.

"Well, Snow, to tell you the truth, neither Langley nor I are here to solve your personal crises outside of work. We would just both like to share with you our hope that you will reach a viable solution that will enable you to continue your association with GROWTH. If you need a few days off to settle personal matters, I'm sure that can be arranged."

I glance at Langley.

"Of course, Snow."

He relaxes, preparing to end the interview.

"My crisis is about the work itself."

They glance at each other and Mary gives me a nod to continue. Together they are now the perfect, impenetrable,

228

parental machine: well-oiled, in absolute sync, aloof from human stinks and crazies. Omnipresent, omniscient and omnipotent, they smile benevolently from Olympus.

"I feel like I'm misusing power. I learn techniques that other people don't know and then by using those techniques I get them to do things. They don't really have a choice."

Langley is feeling confident now, once more my guide, and he dares to unveil his eyes and twinkle at me.

"You are right, Snow, in that you do have more skills. But you are also wrong. Everyone does have a choice here. In this case you just tune in on your Contact's choice a little before she does. You then help her move a bit faster to actualize it. Nobody can choose for another. You are merely an instrument, Snow, not God."

Mary chuckles. "Sometimes we need to remind Langley of that, don't we, Snow?"

He laughs too and they smile at me lovingly.

"I'd like to just say a couple more things."

They nod in unison.

"I don't believe it's true what you say about the ability to know somebody else's choice before they do. It doesn't seem right to me if a person doesn't get there himself. You're teaching us to act like we know more than the next guy, to be some kind of elite force. But, really, everybody's confused, looking for answers. And a person's a liar if he doesn't own up to it. So how can you or anybody else take the right to manipulate another person into something and pretend that it's free will? At least have the decency to call it totalitarianism."

"Snow, dear, you're not making too much sense," says Mary.

I try to slow down my breathing.

"You say the mother signs the contract, she makes a

choice, it's her responsibility. But the thing is, when she signs that piece of paper, it's after a whole symphony that has been designed to lull her into taking the pen and signing her name. And she doesn't know it. She believes that she was awake the whole time, analyzing rationally and making decisions. She doesn't know she was in a semi-trance, programmed into answers and responses. And when I pack up and leave, she goes about proving to herself and her husband that she made a choice here, that she took responsibility. And it's all a big con, a lie. Powerful, conscious techniques were used to stop her powers of thought, of logical deduction, in order to persuade her in a certain direction. It's not her fault that she was manipulated by experts. And even if she realizes she's been had, she feels so guilty that she was stupid and allowed it to happen that even then she won't complain."

I look straight at Langley. His face is no longer loving.

"You're a wee bit paranoid, Snow," he says. "Perhaps it is just as well that you take a break. And thank you for sharing with us."

"Sure. But I want you to know that you haven't ruined the belief inside me. I've been conned, but you haven't turned me into one of yours. You haven't got that much power."

"Snow, dear . . . " Langley stands and shows me to the door. "You're very young, with your whole life ahead of you. I suggest you get some professional counseling to help you plan for the future. You're a bright young woman and not really exploiting your potential. Now please leave your case with Laurie at the desk and best of luck to you."

I take a cab to Ernie.

"I wish I could feel triumphant or something, cutting all my ties, but I don't. I feel like just about everybody's died and I'm left alone after the Atomic Blast."

"Just like you don't want them to lay expectations on you,

you shouldn't lay expectations on them either," says Ernie.

He's right. I can't spend my life trying to make others understand me. It's all I can do to try and figure myself out.

We sit in Ernie's apartment on Lombard Street, the living-room windows overlooking the "crookedest street in the world." He's made lunch: cracked crab in ice and champagne. Sitting on giant cushions at a low wooden table, we eat slowly, checking each other out. His kindly, lined face gives me courage.

"I want to discuss a possible living arrangement with you, Ernie."

He doesn't smile.

"Why?"

"I've thought about it a lot. Of all the people I've met in my life, you're the most opinionated, self-centered and egotistical, and also the most truly gracious. You operate off what feels good to you, not some Cause. It feels good to be around you."

"And if I say no?"

"Then I'll find something by myself."

"Okay then."

"Ernie!"

I jump up and throw my arms around him. He hugs me back.

"Now go and finish the lunch that I so thoughtfully prepared for you. Then take a look at the spare room and decide how you might fix it up. I actually think this arrangement might work out very nicely. My friend can now explain to his wife that he visits us as a couple. We can even go out as a foursome."

"Sure. And I feel better when you let me know I can do something for you too."

He gives me a sharp, deep look.

"You know that's true, Ernie."

He looks down at his crab.

"Yes, I know. You've changed a lot since I saw you wandering around in Macy's."

"I think I'm just as ridiculous as ever, but I don't get pushed around as much. I check things out now. You helped me a lot, you know. You even gave me the idea for my next line of employment."

He reaches out and pats my head.

"And now that you're so smart, just don't forget to turn to a friend sometimes. And I will too. I promise."

CHAPTER 27

"*H*ave you ever done any films before?" asks the ugly little man with the bald head. He has nice eyes, though, and a sweet smile.

"In high school once. I was in a movie about students who turned into ghouls and attacked their teachers. It was even on TV late at night."

"That's fine. Then you're not camera shy. Now you can undress and show me what your body looks like."

I feel totally detached from my nakedness. Pulling my T-shirt over my head and slipping out of my jeans, I become the girl I remember in the mirror at the cabin. She has a job interview that happens to be for a porno movie, and the director wants to see the merchandise. It's no different from taking a typing test or showing encyclopedia samples. I want the job. The pay is good, and it's a good way to get sexual experience in an honest way; no feelings involved and a chance to find out what I like and don't like. Most important, there's no hypocrisy here, no pretense of being anything other than what it is.

"Stand up straight and turn around a couple of times.

Very nice, actually. You have a young girl's body. Good possibilities. You're going to have to lose a couple of pounds, though. My girl will give you some exercises to tighten your thighs and some things for flexibility too. Now tie your hair back into a couple of pigtails and look in that box in the corner for a prop. I'm going to call Harry in to take some pictures."

"Does that mean I get the job?"

"Sure, honey. I'll explain it after we shoot a roll."

"Wait a minute, Mr. Trowel." I pull the T-shirt back on and call him by his last name even though he invited me to call him Malcolm. "How do I know you're not going to go out and use those pictures and that's the last I'll ever hear of you?"

I'm quite proud of my business-like attitude. I can see he admires it too.

"All right, Snow. Let's talk first. Harry wants to get something to eat, so I'll tell him to take pictures when he gets back."

He picks up the phone and asks Harry to bring back sandwiches.

"Look, kid, I'll be straight with you. This is a business like any other business. We've got a growing market for these video things we make, actually more than we can handle. I'm making a good living and it's only going to get better. I don't need to cheat. Everything's legal. We do nice, clean sex films, no violent, weird stuff. We look for the new face, new angle, new turn-on. We sign contracts with our people, say exactly how much you make, and right there in print that you don't have to do anything you don't feel like doing. There's bad people in every business, honey, and you're right to check it out. I'd want my own kid to do the same thing. I'm a family man. For years I had a little shoe store. Now I do video tapes. Just going where the market is. What you should do is talk to some of the other boys and girls who work here and they'll tell you about the place."

"But why do you need to shoot pictures of me now?"

"That's how we put the movie together. We go through the files, see what we got, and build up a plot around the combinations. I also got to see how you photograph. If you'd stop and think for a minute, you'll agree it just doesn't make sense that I'd lure girls in here to sell their pictures on street corners. There's not enough money in it."

It sounds sensible. Besides, what's the worst that can happen? So he sells a few pictures.

Harry comes in with the sandwiches and coffee. He's in his twenties and cute, and I feel shy. But he's all business, putting me at ease, nods and turns to Malcolm to discuss some problems they're having with their film lab. I take my sandwich to finish over by the box of props in the corner. There's a jumble of things inside: whips, a green plastic frog, a brown rubber snake, handcuffs, an all-day sucker in cellophane, a butterfly net, clothesline, ostrich feathers, a trumpet and a Raggedy Ann doll. I choose the Raggedy Ann doll to go with the pigtails.

"You ready, Snow?"

Malcolm Trowel is relaxed and matter-of-fact. Harry turns on overhead lights and sets up his camera on a tripod.

"Good choice. Now just play with that doll like you were a little kid. Talk to her. Read to her. Cuddle her. Be natural and open. Remember we want to see your body so don't hide yourself. On the other hand, don't pose or feel like you've got to exaggerate. Our films are known for their genuine quality, ungross, if you know what I mean. So go ahead, whenever you're ready. Ignore Harry, he'll do his thing and you pretend you're all alone."

I pull off the T-shirt and take the doll over to the chair Harry has placed in front of the camera. As soon as I'm

235

naked I again have that separated feeling, like I'm in a trance and watching from outside. I see myself and the doll. I talk to her and kiss her, throw her up in the air and catch her, and feeling safe and almost sexless, I wipe tears from her eyes and use her cloth hand to wipe mine.

"That's great, kiddo. You can pull your clothes on now. Print it up fast, Harry. We'll have her down tomorrow to take a look at the proofs."

"That was fun."

I sit down in front of his desk, now littered with half-eaten sandwiches and dirty Styrofoam cups.

"Now what?"

"The first thing I want you to do, before you come in tomorrow, is buy some of those white cotton underpants, like the little girls wear. Also get two of those paddle ball things – you know, the ball is attached to the board on elastic. I want you to practise batting with both hands at the same time."

"I understand the underpants."

He laughs. "We're getting into 3-D now and the paddle balls number is something I've been wanting to try out for a while. You're perfect for it. Probably have you chewing some bubble gum too. The majority of stuff you'll be doing will be stunt numbers like that. For the actual sucking and fucking close-ups I've got a special crew who know the tricks. Hey, don't look so disappointed. You watch, honey, and learn. We'll let you do some long-range fucking shots and a little close-up fondling but I just have the feeling you don't know the ropes enough for keeping the guys going. Sometimes we have to shoot and reshoot an angle, it takes forever, and I've got to have girls who can keep a guy hard a really long time. I'm sure you'll learn quickly, though. Now I'll send in Sandy to talk to you about diet and exercise and

I'll see you around ten tomorrow morning. Nice to have met you, Snow."

A few minutes later a woman who looks like a high school vice-principal walks in and skillfully looks me up and down.

"He says you're a fast learner."

Ernie comes home to find me exhausted in the living room, two paddle ball rackets hanging from my limp wrists. We eat cheese and onion pie made from *The Poor Poet's Cookbook*, my having been instructed that anything from that book will meet with Ernie's approval.

"Well, I think it's a great way to make a buck. But you better not tell your women pals about this."

"Some of them would understand, I think. I don't have any Nazi thoughts about it."

"Well, you've got a job that pays well with room for advancement, a home and a good man. I guess it's happily ever after then, isn't it? That is, if the Canadian Dream is anything like the American one."

"Oh, it is, it is."

"Well, welcome to the Castle of Dreams Come True. Now go stretch out on the couch and I'll wash up and make coffee."

So this is happily ever after. This is what happens when you don't find Mr. Right in his flowing cape to take you to magic places that you need his passport to get into. This is my alternate happiness to the washer/dryer unit, mortgage to pay off and a man whose main reason for being is to provide for me. I'm going to just have to reconcile myself to being a dot of light alone in the great darkness, a defective machine that's missing the appropriate coding to relate to the rest of the universe. I guess I can live with that. It's better than being a Nazi.

"Here's Kleenex," says Ernie. "Go ahead and cry. Nobody ever talks about what Cinderella felt after the wedding."

I sniff into the tissue.

"I'm still afraid I need to be hospitalized or something."

"Dear, you've forgotten you're talking to an officially classified disease here. It'll have to get colder than a witch's tit before I'll go turning friends over to the psychiatric establishment. Now you just go on and have yourself a good sniffle, about life or whatever, and Uncle Ernie won't mind a bit."

A few more strangled noises come out of my throat and then there is a shift in gear, like an underground passage opening up inside, and air that's been trapped for a long time rushing to the surface. The sound alone is enough to frighten me into paralysis, but Ernie strokes my head and mutters "That's a good girl" and lets me go on gushing.

After a while, when it seems to be mostly over, he hands me the whole box of Kleenex and turns on the TV, the news and pictures of the victims of Vietnam. A sobbing woman covered with hideous napalm burns fills the screen. And an amazing thing occurs. I look at her in a way I never did before, without guilt that it was my fault it happened or that it should have been me burned instead. I don't even feel her suffering cancels my right to cry. I look at her for a couple of seconds and try to figure out what's happening. And here is what it is. I imagine the two of us together as dots of light in the darkness, both struggling in our own way to find some comfort, somehow united on this planet where all those old rules no longer apply.

About the Author

LISA HERMAN was born in Los Angeles and moved to Toronto with her parents while still an infant. After receiving a B.A. in English from York University, where she was active in theater, she left for San Francisco. She worked at various jobs and lived in various places. She received a second B.A. in Psychology at Berkeley, and an M.Sc. in Counseling at California State University. For five years she worked as a therapist and actress in Los Angeles. In 1978 she emigrated to Israel and worked as a therapist and writer until her return to Toronto in 1988. She is married and the mother of twins. This is her first novel.